ON A PLANET ALIEN is an original POCKET BOOK edition.

Books by Barry N. Malzberg

Beyond Apollo
The Destruction of the Temple
Herovit's World
On a Planet Alien

Published by POCKET BOOKS

BARRY N. MALZBERG

ON A PLANET ALIEN

PUBLISHED BY POCKET BOOKS NEW YORK

ON A PLANET ALIEN

POCKET BOOK edition published October, 1974

L

This original POCKET BOOK edition is printed from brand-new plates made from newly set, clear, easy-to-read type.
POCKET BOOK editions are published by POCKET BOOKS,
a division of Simon & Schuster, Inc., 630 Fifth Avenue,
New York, N.Y. 10020. Trademarks registered
in the United States and other countries.

For Bill Pronzini

FLICKER OF HISTORY: Lying on the bleak earth of this blasted planet, listening to the wind filter through the trees, it is possible for one moment in the clinging darkness to believe that it is not impossibly removed, that it is not at the far edge of the universe but that indeed it is Earth itself and this has not been a voyage outward but a voyage in, to some other aspect of familiar terrain . . . but in the next moment, as Nina comes close against me once more that feeling slides away from me thinly like all illusion and the feeling of *alienness* seeps in once again. It is not Earth, it is nothing we have ever known: we have voyaged at impossible speed to the heart of the unknown . . . and still I lie there, looking up at the impenetrable sky, shaking. My legs seem fibers filled with small tremors. She presses harder.

"Come on, Hans," she says, "stop thinking." Her voice is tentative but underneath is insistence. "There is nothing to think about." She begins to stroke at me. "Come here."

I close my eyes, open them, then roll, clearing that distance between us, drawing her within. There is no flight. She is right; her corporeality makes its own statement: I cannot withdraw from her. Under the rules and terms of the compact she is to be satisfied and I am her coupling: therefore I must satisfy her. Therefore to satisfy her. Slowly I bring my knee up the inner surfaces of her thigh, there is a wicker of contact beneath the cloth that surrounds us, then slowly I roll to cover her all the way, draw my knees up, seeking. In the forest which surrounds us I can

7

hear sounds which might be those of the birds and animals but then again—when this pastoral flight falls away like a garment—it is more likely to be the natives at the rim of the forest, crashing around, peering within. The idea that the natives, not discouraged by our fires, by the walls of insulation which we have placed, might actually be looking within, seeing what Nina and I are doing, fills me with a perverse excitement, a feeling of disconnection and floating to be sure and now the contact between us is no longer so tenuous but indeed wedges hard, wedges harder, and I feel myself beginning to flow within her. *Ah!* she groans, a scatological little moan, *aha, aha!* for all the coldness of her exterior she has always taken a simple and basic pleasure in the act of coupling and I turn myself over to the sensations completely, feeling them beginning to waft around me.

We couple. On the floor of the forest we couple. The old graceless motions overwhelm me and momentarily I am no longer a scientist, no longer Hans the Captain (as I refer to myself in interior monologue) but merely a being caught on the pipe of mortality, flinging myself in and out of her spasmodically. Dragging myself to orgasm like a man moving hand-over-hand on piping, there is, near the peak, a sudden moment of hesitation, a superimposed blankness and then once again that image returns: an image of familiarity oozing into all the crevices of consciousness: this planet is not irretrievably alien, *Nina and I are not light years from home but indeed the two of us are coupling normally in familiar surroundings.* When my orgasm comes it is then on a bright thread of pain: lost, irrevocably lost, a billion years from home only to recover the old sensations which will never, never hurl us back . . . unless of course most of this is taking place in my mind and not on the terrain of what they will come to call Folsom's Planet.

II

EXPOSITORY DATA: My name is Hans Folsom. I am the captain of this expedition. The expedition is therefore known as Folsom's Voyage and the planet will be known, eventually, as Folsom's Planet. The Bureau is quite consistent in these policies and procedures; the commander of the voyage has the right to impose his name if not his will upon the mission. There is no megalomania in this. It is simple justice. At the cost of enormous risks one is entitled, at least, to a small piece of immortality.

There are four on this Folsom's Expedition: Folsom himself, vigorous, cheerful, in the flower of his manhood, his mate Nina, who has already been introduced rather abruptly, and Stark and Closter, about whom more will be said presently. You will hear of them presently; they are also mates in a binding arrangement: the strict pairing as approved by the Bureau indicated that there would be no cross-matching involved. For that reason Stark and Closter, despite the fact that they are under my command, stay pretty much to themselves in one area while Nina and I, of course, manage to make our connections in another.

Folsom's Planet itself is some eighty-three million miles from its sun, that sun (which perhaps shall be known as Folsom's Star) being located some thirty-seven hundred and twelve light years from the earth. An appalling distance, to be sure, but the explosion of technological sophistication, the postindustrial revolution, so to speak, has resulted in devices which enabled us to make this transversion in a mere three and a half years (I cannot give you the exact calculations since we were asleep for most of the time) and by the time we are to return this may be even further reduced.

Our function is to civilize the natives of Folsom's Planet after, of course, having made contact with them. Specographic probe of the planet conducted from 2417 through 2429 established the presence on the planet of intelligent life at stage three of sophistication, still bound to the ecology but at the beginnings of a crude technology. Optimistically, this is the best time at which contact should be made with aliens; if they fall below the stage three level, they are apt to be hesitant or unduly hostile, communication is difficult to establish; beyond stage three, clear up to six and seven, often even moving up to eight, paranoia begins to intervene: they are skeptical about the motives of the Federation and often inexcusably hostile.

What does the Federation have to gain by establishing communication, advancing their technology? they want to know.

Exactly why are emissaries being sent from a distant star to give them the intellectual and technological materials to join this Federation?

What, strictly speaking, is in it for them?

This is why all efforts are made to avoid the six and seven civilizations to say nothing of the duller and more pedestrian one's and two's: no, the three's are proper, being at that right area between numb credulity and resistance.

We will spend approximately one year on Folsom's Planet. After establishing communication with the natives, a task which with sophisticated linguistic devices takes usually no more than a matter of days, we will proceed, through philosophical and technological orientation lectures to place skills in their hands, one by one as if they were implements. By these means they may take their rightful place amidst the races of the stars; having done this, we will leave the planet for the somnolent return journey to the Earth but our narcoticized dreams all the way back will be drenched

10

with the feeling of fulfillment: we will have done our part to civilize the universe, to tame the forces of entropy; we will have placed within the hands of this race the means by which they can acquire skills to match our own . . . and in due time, when they create their first starship, when they voyage solemnly to the Pit in which the races themselves are gathered, when they enter the Ceremony of Music . . . when they do this it will not only be a celebration of Folsom's Planet but of Folsom himself, that skillful voyager who carried forth to them the implements by which they could take their place in the Federation.

At least that was the point and purpose of the voyage; that is, so to speak, the plan, but we are in severe difficulties of a sort which never could have been pondered before our landing and at this time the modus operandi, that simple, pure, elegant, almost compositionally architectured modus operandi which has applied to the settlement of stage three planets since the beginning of process . . . that modus operandi lies in ruins. My fornicative activities, my glossy ruts with Nina are, in fact, one of the few comforts which I have been able to derive thus far from Folsom's Planet.

For one thing, we cannot establish any contact with the natives.

And for another, I am not in the least sure that even if we did, they would want any part of the marvelous devices and advances which we can offer them.

From the little information which we can gather, their attitude, in fact, appears to be uniquely hostile.

III

BRINGING THE GOOD NEWS: Nevertheless, Closter and I, laden with equipment, set to once again on our lumbering walk to the edges of the forest and that point at which the habitats of the natives begin. We are laden with gifts; the standard trinkets, jewelry, intoxicants, ornaments dangle glistening from our belts as we lurch through the belt of trees toward the open spaces.

The air of the planet caresses us as we stride forward, the sensation is as if open palms were rubbing across our cheeks. Always the bucolic, pastoral, enveloping atmosphere of Folsom's Planet is a surprise; it was selected, of course, for the commodiousness of its environment, for the ability of Earth-type peoples to walk on the terrain without artificial assist of any sort: neither helmet nor support devices of any kind are required. We knew all of this before we embarked, how good the conditions were on Folsom's Planet that is to say, but even so, it was jolting to emerge from the cramped spaces of the ship to find, after our years of dreams and confinement, this situation. Debarkation is in itself a kind of miracle; this is one of my epigrams.

"Do you see them?" Stark says. He pauses, shades his eyes, gestures toward an opening in the trees where dimly we can see forms moving. "There they are." He wipes a large hand across his forehead, shakes his head, comes to a halt. "I just don't know if I can face this again," he says.

"You'll face it," I say grimly enough. Stark is the sociotechnician among us; it is he who is responsible for the alignments between the crew and the natives, the delicate network of interrelationships which will be established; it is also his responsibility to graph and plot out the lines of connection within the natives' society itself which by implication will make all of their societies visible. So far he has been running into very bad luck—for one thing we have been utterly unable to make any contact with the natives whatsoever—and this bad luck has made him unpleasant, contributed to our own deterorating relationship.

"You'll face this exactly the same as we will," I add and motion toward him to start moving again. His eyes close; his forehead dampens and some aspect of light makes it look like a fist as he moans and moves forward once again. "I don't think you understand, Hans," he says, "I don't think you understand the seriousness of this situation."

"I understand it very well."

"You couldn't possibly. No one not in the specialty could. We've been unable to establish contact, we're getting resistance at levels which cannot even be articulated and furthermore, *oh* . . ."

He stops. Talking as we have been moving, we break through a clearing, find that we are standing on a small cliff, overlooking a primitive settlement. The natives move amidst huts which are poised on a large square; in that square there is a large smoking pot, a few horses tethered and sleeping and a small, squabbling crowd in the center which might indicate commerce. As they see us they begin to look upwards: all movement in the square stops and from the huts themselves other heads move forward and we walk into the solemn, ungiving stares of forty or fifty of the natives. It is perhaps the unanimity of those stares which has brought the *oh* from Stark's lips but then again it may be something else; I am utterly unable to understand him. I have never claimed that insight was my strength; I depend instead wholly upon observation.

"Oh," Stark says again and stands on that cliff, his

13

features wavering as if in the breeze, "oh my, they're looking again but what are we going to do? There must be some way to reach them."

His little mouth furrows with concentration, then he steps forward, making a series of gestures, the universal gestures of communication which the Bureau has carefully transcribed. Below there seems to be a sigh; a cast of wind blowing through the assemblage and then the natives, almost insolently, break from their frieze and begin to resume their tasks again. The square moves with a torpid life. One wizened native crouching near a corner hut fixes us with a long, gleaming gaze which seems to carry all implication within it, then takes a stick, throws it in our direction and turns. The stick, caught by the breezes, floats in the air, turns, lands downrange about three feet from our position. Stark shakes his head.

"They're making fools of us," he says.

"It has nothing to do with us."

"They're laughing at us. They're thwarting all of our efforts to achieve communication."

"Don't take it personally," I say. "It's a question of their own ethos."

"So what are we supposed to do?" Stark says. He turns toward me, his face blotched with high, strained lines of sweat. "Go on with this? Allow them to make fools of us? There has got to be some end to this."

"Enough," I say.

I touch him on the shoulder, pull him around. He looks at me, the little spaces of his face caving in toward one another: in the cracks there is oozing, or perhaps this is merely some trick of light. Our instructions, our procedures, of course, are very rigid: we are not to force communication. If normal attempts at bridging as laid out in the procedural manuals do not work we are to lay back, wait for contacts to be initiated by the culture itself. This, according to the policies and procedures, is inevitable. But then, according to those same policies and procedures, contact has never been, cannot conceivably be, refused.

Obviously we are in difficulties but Stark is merely compounding them.

"Let's go back."

Stark shakes his head. His face is old, ravaged.

"How long is this going to go on? How long is it going to be this way?"

"Until we initiate contact."

"How long are we going to be in this accursed place?" He seems on the verge of losing control. "All of my graphs, my charts, our maps, our schemes . . . are they going to come to nothing?" His voice wavers, breaks rather dramatically. He totters against me, turns, begins to reel back into the forest. "It's not right," he says but permits me weakly to lead him away from the clearing. He lurches against me for comfort. I feel some dull abcess of compassion opening within me as he falls against me, a sudden and unwanted sympathy and I push this away almost as violently as I impel Stark himself from me: I cannot afford feeling, I am the commander. "It's not right," he says again without energy and lolls against a tree, his frame slumping there in an aqueous fashion before with a constriction of limbs he forces himself from that limb and propels himself toward me. "All right," he says, "let's go back then."

"We have no choice."

"We'll never establish contact. We'll never be able to get through to them at all."

"Be of good will," I say. "Do not be discouraged. Eventually contact will be made. Contact has never failed in the history of all the expeditions. It will not fail this time."

He shakes his head: a nest of trinkets at his belt catches a bolt of sun, glistens. He squeezes his eyes shut, then seems to expand them. "You are a fool," he says.

"That is insubordination," I say. I put a hand on his shoulder to impel him through the forest but suddenly I feel a stab of disgust. What after all is the point? We will go prowling back through the wretched forest and find ourselves once again at the ship. From ship through forest to natives. Natives to forest to ship. Nothing will break that circuit. "I am not a fool," I say.

"Certainly you are a fool," Stark says without energy. But his eyes, widening still, are very bright. "You think that this is like all of the other missions and that everything will work out well. Just because something has always happened one way you think it will continue to happen. That is a failure of logic."

"Logic will not fail. By definition it cannot."

"Then you do not," Stark says rather wildly, "then you do not understand logic," and there are sounds behind us, heaving and crashing within the forest. Instantly galvanized to action I turn; Stark turns as well, the two of us poised to alertness as even without our conscious guidance the subconscious training of the team comes to the fore. We drop to protective positions, I clamber within my clothing for the weapon secreted within. Arched in that position it is as if for a moment that we are not in the forest of Folsom's Planet but in some prehistoric vault of the mind, some concavity in which all emotions come free to stalk and a wind which is not wholly of the planet's making burrows its way through us. My fingers curl more tightly around the weapon, an incendiary which can render apart anything, living or dead, within a range of some fifty yards, and as I do so, with some other portion of my alert, compartmentalized commander's mind I can see that Stark has remitted to a kind of sheer terror, his hands gripping one another, his face sliding toward a perfect whiteness. His lips open and close spasmodically. I turn toward the source of the crashing and see then through an opening in the branches one of the natives, probably an Elder, a shrunken male wearing loose clothing, his mouth open, his face constricted in some parody of Stark's own expression and as he moves toward me he catches sight of the weapon: suddenly he halts, extends his hand and then falls to a crouched position. His eyes are glazed with fright but he holds himself steady, his limbs locked toward frieze.

16

Slowly I extend my hand, take the weapon from Stark's grasp, put it into my clothing. He stands there contemplating the native. Slowly, in his crouched position, the native extends his hands still further and begins to make strange hawking sounds which have, yet, the pattern and regularity of speech.

"Do you see?" I say to Stark who is still breathing unevenly, his breath rasping. "Do you see now?"

"See what?" he says, looking down at the Elder who stares up at Stark in some reflection of that expression until I can make the equation; in some dark way Stark and the Elder are the same. They mirror parts of one another. For all the eternal separateness of the races there is still, according to all the principles of the Federation, a similarity.

"Communication has been established," I say.

And the native, as if understanding, nods joyously.

IV

POLICIES AND PROCEDURES: For three years
in transport to Folsom's Planet we lived as if under
the gauze of a dream, the thick blanket of somnolence
lying over us as on automatic the ship hurled itself
outward. Every six months one of us would be arisen
by the machinery for a period of three days to tend
the ship, to make sure that the converters were working properly, to re-establish communications with the
Bureau, to make sure that the life support processes
continued as previously. These duties were shared
and thus it was only necessary to arise once through
the course of the three years meaning that only three
days were stripped from my own chronology by duties. The Bureau is thoughtful and considerate about
this. The Bureau understands that life is precious, time
its only ingredient, and that if we were forced to ex-
pend much more of it than that minimum three days
there would be even less enthusiasm for the probes
than there has been already. The probes, as they are,
are a difficult enough situation: one must leave family,
friends, life, work to spend some seven or eight years
away from all of them in the establishment of a bridge-
head with backward races; returning to the Earth after
that lapse means that life has so severely changed that
it is almost impossible, outside of the controlled life
of the Bureau, to enter into it. If on top of this dislocation the penalty of lost years were also imposed,
it is possible that the only staff the Bureau could find
for the probes would be misfits, those who would be
just as happy to have no contact with the outer culture at all.

That would be bad of course. If we are to bring the fruits of our civilization to backward races (who, perhaps, I will refer to in the future as *br*'s for economy of space; there is only so much room in the transmission belt) then it stands to reason that the carriers should be those splendidly adopted to the society, equally well adopted to the rigors of the Federation and its obligation to carry the word of union to the furthermost race . . . but those splendidly well-adjusted personnel would object to losing one tenth or more of their irreplaceable lives sitting in the small space of bulkheads, listening to the transistors hum. No, it is necessary for the Sleep to be imposed so at least none of the juices of mortality are expended during the great voyage. But alone in the ship at my own interval, two and a quarter years deep into the voyage, I could feel the stirring of animals deep in the network, the sounds of forces so great that I could not even apprehend them and after a brief look at my sleeping companions (Stark and Closter side by side in their room, their bodies disgustingly intertwined as they had requested; Nina lying in a position made almost lascivious by unconsciousness, her limbs disjointed, falling open, her mouth pursed in an *O* that might have been a cry or a kiss, and though slack with disuse the slow muscles of desire nevertheless contracted within me) I ascertained that the sounds were not caused by them and that they had no reference at all to these other bodies in the ship. I wandered into the control room, that small and vital stage in the midst of machinery that carried the ship ever deeper into the night and there at the heart of the transistors.

I looked into the blank and empty spaces of the universe which surrounded us like a blanket, and swaddled then within I asked, "Why have we come out here? Why are we carrying the good news of technology and integration to the natives of Folsom's Planet? Is there any need for this? What is the source of the missionary impulse?"

Because it must be done, a voice which might

19

have been my own answered. Perhaps it was not my own. Perhaps it was some other presence in the ship although if this were so, this flat projection would have indicated that I was insane and I do not think of myself as being insane. Not yet. Not just yet. Do not question the missionary impulse, the voice said. Consider only what must be done.

"Three years," I said, listening to the whir and the whine. "Three years out and three years back; a year or more in settlement on a planet we have never seen and for what?" I was rather self-pitying. Two years in suspended animation will do this to one; it seeps the joints with the humours of self-pity in an almost metaphysical fashion. "There must be some reason for this, above and beyond the simple fact of being. Am I right?"

The Federation reigns supreme, the voice pointed out. The Federation consists of all the known races of intelligence living together in harmony and trust. Races which show primitive intelligence but have not been absorbed into the Federation must be for their own protection. If not, they might emerge into savagery and barbarism, attack the Federation with great weapons which were beyond their true means to control. They would have to be eliminated, billions upon billions of sentient creatures. Better to absorb them into the Federation.

"That's easy enough for you to say," I responded. The ship took a dislocative lurch: a feeling of tumbling and revolving slowly in weightlessness came over me. I began to feel a loose sense of easy disconnection burbling through me along with the self-pity, an aqueous twitch to the joints. How I revolved in the air! Yet my little mouth continued to emit its peeping and protesting syllables. The urge of man to establish his will even in the most perverse circumstances is remarkable. "After all you're merely a voice. You bear no responsibility. I do. I'm the captain. This is Folsom's Voyage. We are going to Folsom's Planet."

Go back into suspension, the voice said.

"I can't do that. You know that as well as I do; I've got to remain conscious for three twenty-four hour cycles. That's part of the policies and procedures." I had managed to stabilize, tightened my wrists and elbows around my knees, managed further to cease the rotation so that I floated like a fetus in the clear dim light of the hatch, the walls closing in on me. "Anyway, I don't believe in you. You're just a voice. Go away."

You started this, the voice said rather petulantly. I was just going about my business being the spirit of the ship; you were the one who started this discussion. Personally I don't care whether you talk to me or not. I've got my own tasks.

"Maybe the natives of Folsom's Planet feel the same way about us," I said suddenly, stricken by an idea, that idea, the first one in two years and three months assuming proportions of excitement that were, perhaps, somewhat beyond its legitimate due. "Maybe they don't want to be interfered with. What right do we have to impose upon them? That's what I'd like to know. For that matter what right do we have to call it Folsom's Planet? They don't call it that I'm sure. Even though," I added with a certain amount of pride, "it is going to be known, of course, as Folsom's Planet through the rest of eternity."

Indeed, the voice agreed, so there's your answer right there.

"What? What answer?"

The answer to your question. Why is the Federation imposing its will upon Folsom's Planet? So that it can *be* Folsom's Planet, safe throughout the rest of eternity, fulfilling its place in the great and peaceful confederation of all the races of Man.

"Circular," I said vaguely, "that strikes me as being rather circular reasoning; that seems to be a flaw of logic, saying that the purpose of this is to incorporate Folsom's Planet into the great and peaceful confederation of all the races of Man when really it's the federation of all the races of Man which wants to incorporate Folsom's *Planet*. If you see what I mean,"

I said and gulped rather indelicately, feeling a sudden surge of revulsion, a contraction of the intestines sending a sheer stream of bile through the anterior portions of the intestine and then up by degrees into the cavities of the chest, into the esophagus itself. "Excuse me," I said, "I feel rather ill."

That's all right, the voice said, you can be as ill as you want, it has nothing to do with the essential situation.

But too late, too late, whirling in the air, the weightlessness impinging upon me, I could feel the quiverings and the quaverings of the stomach and underneath that, the understanding that I might evacuate; there was the danger of vomiting under the state of weightlessness of which we had all been apprised before the voyage, and which our training itself had made additionally clear. Vomiting in weightlessness equalled suffocation and so I concentrated desperately upon holding my gorge within me, revolving slowly, holding myself together, and all thoughts of the expedition, of our obligations to the natives of Folsom's Planet, of the ethicality of the mission itself were subsumed in this larger necessity to control myself. No thoughts of the foundation, no thoughts as well of the other sleepers in the ship, nor of the hum from the transistors: the only thought being of control itself, the holding within and spinning then in the dank air deprived of gravitation. I feel unconscious overwhelming me once again, not an unconsciousness this time of the sedatives and the machinery which have controlled me but rather the sheer blank of dislocation, overwhelming, humming with the transistors, and at the center of this perhaps is some understanding of what or who the voice might have been . . . but there is no time to think of that at all as the powerful and deadly machines carry me to that mystery known as Folsom's Planet where all, at last, will begin.

V

THE FOLSOM BLUES: After Stark and I have returned to our encampment, the Elder trailing behind us muttering small, unheard confidences to the wind, after that same Elder has been placed in rude and hastily constructed quarters which adjoin our own but are walled off from them by protective devises, after I have held a brief explicatory meeting in which the other three have been informed of our abortive attempt to make contact once again and the sudden decision of the native to return with us, after Nina has retired to our tent and Stark to the one he shares with Closter, after the alien has been lulled into somnolence with the fruits and small gifts which we have been instructed to give them, Closter approaches me by the fire where I am sitting, meditating upon all of the events of the day and without being asked, kneels near, his joints trembling. Looking at him in the flickers and flashes of light, I am reminded once again of his similarity to Stark, how much they look like one another; I wonder if the rituals of bonding have to do with this similarity which pre-existed or if, more interestingly, that similarity is an outcome of the bonding process.

Closter, the geologist on the voyage, remains deferential after he has assumed his posture but under his silence, that deference is the clear and dull insistence of one who will be heard; I know that if I do not permit him to address me a confrontation of some sort will develop. In part, this is one of the tactics of the strong leader: to evaluate the implications of all circumstance. If Closter were not charged to my care

23

I would not have to be concerned with his moods but since he is, his moods are the object of obsessive interest. Under all circumstances, the mission must be preserved. Thinking of this, realizing my dedication to a mission which in many ways I have already come to repudiate, I have a brief and searing moment of introspection: am I insane? Am I misjudging circumstance? Am I taking all of this, perhaps, too seriously? But that would be impossible; by the very dictates of the Bureau my judgments are absolute and therefore to be trusted.

"They consist," Closter says to me, beginning as he so often does in mid-argument; there is very little sense of exposition or development with Closter's arguments, they are simply there, all of a piece and to enter his world is to enter his rhetoric, "they consist of an agrarian society bound together by mythic elements, the mythic elements themselves coming out of their connection to the land. They have little taste for abstraction: these myths of which I speak cannot be said to be systematized but instead come from common elements: the weather, the cycles of the season, the appearance of vegetation and so on. This is quite characteristic of a society at this stage of development, pretechnological that is to say."

"That is to say," I echo rather mindlessly, looking at the sun setting in the distance, disappearing behind clouds of that very vegetation in the distance, the red cast of that sun bringing to me memories of old Earth and indeed rather inflaming me with nostalgia. The Bureau concentrates upon finding planets, civilizations, atmospheres compatible with our own biology: still the similarities between Folsom's Planet and that idealized Earth of retrospect are almost uncanny. If I were to close my eyes I would believe in fact that I were back upon the Earth, breezes bringing me home to memory . . . but I will not close my eyes, rather I fling them open to attention, "but then again what is there to say?" I turn toward Closter rather bemused, little flickers of irritation breaking my attention. Although his presence in the expedi-

24

tion is justified, although his bonding with Stark means that he need concern me little, I still (and I say this frankly) cannot stand the man. Perhaps this has to do with his rather academic and pedantic tone. I would not want to think that it is because he is a homosexual. Stark, after all, is a homosexual: both of them are homosexuals and Stark does not bother me at all. Sexuality is merely an extension of personality; a quirk or trait like the way in which one postures or shows preference for diet. Still, why does Closter irritate me so much? I think of Nina, a little tendril of lust streaking its way across the pane of consciousness and then slowly I adjust myself, become poised. I must go back. I must go back to her even though she is sleeping.

"Still," Closter is saying, "there is this difficulty."

"What difficulty? Difficulty with the native?"

"No. The native is fine. He is sleeping, we have prepared an enclosure for him; he rests comfortably. Furthermore, we are already in communication. He is eager to learn. He will cooperate. No, it is difficulty with the ethos."

"I don't think I understand you."

"The *ethos*," Closter says, "difficulty with the ethos, their dreams, their fixations. The myths should be simple, agrarian, mere extensions of their limited environment . . . and yet they are not. There are elements of a strong monotheism here; the belief in a single and omnipotent deity which is almost unknown at this level of tribal consciousness. Also, the myths are very specific as to the appearance of the God, his manifestation, the origin of their world, the various ways in which the inhabitants fell from the state of grace . . . all of the common elements in short seem to have been somehow compressed and accelerated so that they manage to embrace both more and less than they should."

"I still don't understand," I say. I have no interest in this as well but that would not be a commander's place to say; the welfare of my little crew is my responsibility and this means that all which concerns them must concern me; I must take an interest in all of their little problems no matter how superficial they might be. "But why does this concern you so much?"

"Because it must," Closter says rather sharply, far more sharply than I would have suspected, "because the disparity between the simple, tribal, pretechnological culture and the highly sophisticated myths is absolute. It is inexplicable. Throughout all of our contacts, in the whole history of the Federation itself, we have never come upon a race previously whose myths and culture were not mutually supportive. This cannot be."

"Why?" I say and stretch out my legs, poised in position, still fixated on the sunset. "And why should this matter concern a geologist?"

Closter sighs. "Everything concerns a geologist."

"But what you are talking about is sociological. That would be Stark's material. How come he hasn't discussed this with me?" and then an insight lances and I say, "unless he asked you to do so. Unless he didn't want to discuss this himself."

Closter sighs again. "It did seem that it would be better for me to bring it up than him." He leans back shaking his head. "There was a certain reluctance to discuss anything with you."

"But why?" I say, "why should that be?" And now the native in his enclosure screams, he has been screaming at intervals for some time now, one high piercing shriek followed by sobs and then a collapse to silence: the screams are like those of an animal except that there are no animals as far as we can see in this section of Folsom's Planet, and no fauna at all. At the sound, as if it were a dart impacted into consciousness, Closter turns, shudders, then returns his attention with difficulty to me, the scream meanwhile extending, moving on a bright, red flowering thread, arcing up in the scale and finally Closter says, "I can't stand this any more, I just can't take it," and arching himself upward, his hands and knees like a bow, he moves into a scrambling run toward the na-

26

tive. Slowly I come to my feet, follow him: the native's screams have not discomfited me this much and I would rather continue the discussion with Closter, find out, at the least, why he has been put up to this by Stark but the screams are indeed overwhelming, Closter was right in that regard: these are not the ordinary cries with which the native has responded to his circumstances intermittently for the past several hours but are cries which have instead risen to a real urgency, a stricken terror on which I find myself impaled.

Coming close to the enclosure in which the native has been placed, I see that Stark and Nina are already there, outside the rude opening which has been carved, the two of them bearing the stricken expressions of those who have been possessed by the incomprehensible and cannot bear to come to grips with it. Stark's face looks as if it has been whipped to pallor; with every scream it is as if a jolt of pain moves through him, condensing and Nina, although calmer, has to support herself with a hand against the side of the enclosure in order to maintain her position. As she sees me she beckons toward me in a gesture simultaneously so desperate and vulnerable that I feel myself touched; would almost plunge within the enclosure to bring an end to those screams no matter what the penalty, but it is Closter's hand which restrains me as I move upon the earthen walls, shaking me into a simulacrum of containment, and the screams as if in response seem to modulate, wavering toward regularity. Stark sinks into a crouch, taps one of the walls, then turns toward me showing me his hands, the palms wet. "It's my fault," he says. "It's all my fault."

"What is it?"

"I shouldn't have done it," Stark says, "I shouldn't have done it," and begins to shake in position, his knees colliding with one another and it is Closter who closes the ground upon him and brings Stark to a standing position, extending an arm, forcing Stark into flapping attention against one of the walls. Stark's eyes are dazed and yet curiously submissive in this aspect as if he were submitting to Closter's brutality almost joyfully, his due. He gasps, his body sways. Closter hits him broadhanded across the face, then once more and Stark takes the slaps with an *ah!,* then straightens up rigidly once again. Nina extends a hand and I take it, feel that closing warmth around my palm. "I'm sorry," Stark says, "I tell you, I'm sorry."

"What did you do?" Closter says. "What did you do?" and Stark leans forward as if to answer, it really looks now as if he is going to answer and then the native itself suddenly appears, looking through an opening in the enclosure at eye level. For all the terror of his screams his face appears to be in a slack and perfect repose, the eyes cunning, measuring. We realize now that the screams have stopped. The alien looks through the opening and in this silence the four of us turn our attention toward him, feeling a certain rivetting sense of connection which passes almost as if in a palpable beam of light between us. Stark is quiet now, his fit over; he lies submissive against Closter, lolling in his grasp and then, almost tenderly Closter hits him again, drawing a thin bark of surprise from Stark as he slumps over. The alien peers out at us, his mouth opening and closing repetitively and then words begin to emerge from him: palpable, distinguishable words emerge from that mouth and it is with the feeling then of time commencing that I listen to him.

"I want to learn," the alien says. "I want to learn." The syllables are harsh but distinct. *Wa-ant to ler-n. Wa-ant to ler-n.*

Closter turns toward me.

"Now it begins," he says.

VI

THE ARTIFACTS: On a day not far from then Folsom goes alone to the village beyond the clearing. Now that communication has been established with the alien everything proceeds apace; even Stark and Closter, it seems, have resolved their tensions in the new task of exploring with the alien the facets of his culture, explaining to him our own purposes. Nina the linguist is, of course, deeply involved with this and the first, tentative experiments which are being run, leaving Folsom with more time, more idleness, perhaps, than he would have thought that the commander of the expedition would have. Resultantly he resolves to go to the village alone. Perhaps he will see something worth discovering. Perhaps he will make contact with a native of his own. Folsom's real problem is that he feels at loose ends and left out of the process although, of course, he would never admit this, least of all to himself. Much of what Folsom has discovered comes back, rather in flashes of retrospection.

Folsom did not expect matters to develop in this way. He did not think that the expedition would leave him essentially on the periphery of its purposes. Part of this has to do with the fact that he is not an introspective man, a good quality for a commander but a bad one, perhaps, for one who is now living in alien quarters. Folsom, assigned by the Bureau after years of preparation to be the commander of this voyage, expected something rather different: dim visions of quest stirred in his blood, a dream of "victory" over the aliens whom he somehow thought

29

of as representing a sinister, alien force. These kind of easy, paranoiac shifts are quite common in the thinking of those who have the mentality of the command post: Folsom has a good deal of insight, he is not aware of all of his condition but he is aware of a good part of it. Striding through the forest, moving toward the village where the natives could once again be glimpsed going about their alien and repetitive tasks Folsom indulged himself in a fantasy: that he would be able to find some universal language, a universal source of communication that would be able to establish direct communication with the natives without all those laborious devices with which Stark, Closter and Nina were working upon the captive Elder. Folsom, no linguist he, would be able to establish a direct communicative link. He would speak with the assembled natives, he would inform them of the purpose of the mission, the beneficent goals of the Federation and they would nod with a solemn and joyous understanding. Yes, they would say to Folsom, similarly speaking in universal tongue, yes, that is exactly right. That is exactly the way that we glimpse things as well. Thank you very much for bringing this to our attention. They would invite Folsom to sit in the center of their fires, they would come one by one to tender him with shyness and bring him trusting gifts, they would kneel at his feet while he explained to them the history and condition of the Bureau to say nothing of many interesting personal anecdotes from his own past. The natives would nod with delight and encourage him to tell more. Eventually aliens and Folsom would join in a clamp of trust: Folsom would then convey the band back, perhaps two hundred of them, to the clearing in the forest where the others of the expedition were working on the Elder and would show them exactly what he had accomplished. You see, he would say, as the natives stood behind him beaming and chattering, all of this was unnecessary. All that I had to do was to talk reasonably to them and they responded. You have made far more of this than was truly necessary. There

30

was never any difficulty whatsoever. You should have listened to and trusted me from the first.

Yes, that is what Folsom has in mind, some easy triumph which will restore in a twinkling his command position (he admits that he is feeling somewhat displaced after the capture of the native, the beginning of communication; he has lost his old centrality and influence) but the colder, bolder, saner part of his mind informs him that this will not be so and that he is engaging in fantasy: the natives will give him nothing. They will yield him no more than they have yielded any of them in the past, all except the one that willingly followed: they will retreat to their dwellings, look at Folsom with hostility, make menacing gestures. They will do everything in fact except physically attack him. That is all for the best. Folsom is loaded with incendiary devices, weaponry of various sorts, canisters of poison gasses which if flung would destroy the atmosphere of the planet for a thousand years. Furthermore he is fully authorized to use them; instructions on this point were most explicit. Within his sole judgment is the decision as to how to quell alien attacks if they should develop. Of course it is not expected that they will. They never have.

Stumbling through the forest, little patches and snatches of song bubble through Folsom's consciousness, memories as well of Nina moving against him on the floor of the forest before she became involved with the communications effort. He realizes that he is probably jealous. Underneath the patches and snatches of song, however, hymns that the Bureau itself made part of its training, is something more profound, dream-memories like fish filtering through that screen of unconscious so that he can in small glimpses remember how it might have been, lying in stasis, for two and a half years during the voyage. Something to do with pain, violent, irretrievable pain as if a cosmic bolt had struck the ship, causing it to sway in the void for several minutes or weeks, the vats in which Folsom and his companions were encased churning violently with the force of that unknown impact. For just a moment Folsom thinks that he can literally get hold of it; that he can remember what it was that he is trying to recover in that tank of memory but then, piscine, it slips away through the fumbling hands of his memory, deserting him. He comes from the forest, stands on a high place then, looking down upon the village. The natives are not in sight; it is still dawn, near dawn anyway, the natives probably asleep safely in those tentlike structures or mumbling prayers in their unknown language to some god. Perhaps they think that Folsom is God.

This gives him a twitch of amusement, the conception that they might think of him, of the expedition, as gods, and Folsom allows himself to smile thinly. It is common, the Bureau has advised, for stage three cultures to react to the invaders from the far places in a fashion both mystical and religious and it is quite likely that, awe of gods being one of the primary facets of primitive cultures, they might regard Folsom and his expedition in exactly that way. On the other hand they might not, they might think of them as devils—this is also possible, the Bureau has advised, although not as likely—in which case Folsom can hardly stand self-congratulation.

Looking down at the village he has, in any event, a proprietary feeling, much the feeling that a god *might* have looking upon something in the well of the world, in the well of his own unconscious. This is his planet, these must therefore be his people, whether they respond to him or not, these unthinking primitives are within his province and tutelage; they are his responsibility. Folsom's chest expands. Really, he had never thought of the matter in quite this way: they are his children, he is their keeper, they are his subjects, he is their king, he is their shepherd, they are his flock . . . his interest in them is proprietary. For all of their faults, for all of their stubbornness, their resistance, they are in his charge and in the future, at some awful date in the infinite future when they have taken their place within the

Federation as responsible and contributing members they will look upon him, Hans Folsom, as their father. Throughout eternity this will be known as Folsom's Planet, Folsom himself will be the Founder. This knowledge, this new way of looking at things moves Folsom beyond pride to tears, he feels that flash of humility which has always overtaken him at important moments of accomplishment in his life and he reels forward one step, reels forward another, takes a third toward his destination, his village, and his ankle turns on something, catches a stone buried in the earth and he falls in an undignified spread-eagling fashion, his nose working its way into the dirt, his tall, handsome frame wrenched in an undignified way.

"Son of a bitch!" Folsom says.

Suddenly breathless, not at all hurt (if nothing else his training has taught him how to take a fall correctly) but shaken up, he feels a deep flush of humiliation overtaking him, seeming to start in the space between his shoulder blades, then working down in small, opening circles through his back, spreading into his gaunt, handsome frame. He is afraid, Folsom is, that he might have been seen, that his undignified tumble might have been somehow witnessed within the village (he is in quite a conspicuous position) but a quick, verifying glance below shows him that it has not. The square remains vacant. He begins, then, on hands and knees, keeping his burning face averted from any spectator who might be in a hut or embankment, to look for the source of his tumble and finds it then—a large rock, half buried, half exposed in the earth, gray slate, about two feet across and a foot high in the revealed section, glinting at him in little swatches of sun.

Peculiar, Folsom thinks, peculiar that he has never seen this rock before. He has, after all, been on this rise; he has made several hikes to the village and it is strange that he would not have noticed this. Certainly it is conspicuous, it is hardly something that would have evaded his attention before (even though he had not seen it to stumble upon it this time) but its position deep in the mud, flecked with streaks of dirt upon it, would indicate that it is not new. It must have been here all the time; it does not give indication of having suddenly been dropped into position. The natives would not ambush this position . . . would they?

Interested, Folsom runs his hand over the rock. It has a smooth, fascinating feeling coming underneath his splayed palms, a strange and comforting warmth which surges through the blank surfaces into his fingers, and embarrassed at the luxuriance of the sensations, the close to sensuous feeling which they impart, he looks up, his features suddenly feline with suspicion, casts hurried glances to the right and left, down the embankment to see that he is definitely unobserved, to make sure that no one is witnessing his pleasure . . . and then with an almost imperceptible little grunt, Folsom gives himself over to the rock completely, fluttering his palms up and down its surfaces, enjoying the sheen, his fingers shaking, his arms themselves vibrating in sympathy as he absorbs the warmth pouring in little waves from the rock and then delicately, working on it as a man might tug a ripe fruit from its peeling, he begins to work it to and fro to free it from the earth.

It feels so *good,* that it is the embarrassment, the source of his little cries. Folsom could not have imagined the simplicity and warmth of the sensations which the rock has given him. Sex with Nina is not to be minimized, particularly as it has been sanctified by the mating bond; he is not denying either some of the very sensuous experiences he has had in his lifetime . . . but it is the *unexpectedness* of what the rock gives him, the jarringly out-of-context nature of his pleasure which fills him with something near a dark glee. Unprepared for delight, he has found it. Inured by his commander's role to all sensation, he has been overcome by it. Humming once again, a new song filling his mouth, emerging in parched hoarse whispers as if from the inmost part of it, Fol-

34

som continues his struggles with this rock. He must dislodge it. He must find out its true proportions.

What can it be? He does not know; it is curiosity mingling with the pleasure which drives him through his efforts. The smoothness and warmth of the rock do not decrease but instead seem to heighten as he works his hand through the earth to the undiscovered parts of it, trying to get a hold underneath, palms slipping . . . and as these undiscovered parts lurch against his hands each of them imparts a sensual message of their own, much as the suddenly revealed parts of a woman's body, Folsom thinks, each delivers its message in turn. Grunting, his palms already beginning to become damp in the drenched air of morning, he slides his hands to the elbows underneath the earth and as he works his way through finally he finds some end to the rock; it seems to terminate about three feet below the surface. Frantic with a desire which he cannot even name, Folsom digs his other hand through the soft, dense mire of his planet, his hands meeting underneath the rock in an obscure and tormenting clasp, embracing one another, and closing his eyes, contracting his hard, impressively flat commander's stomach, Folsom inhales once and then uses all of his strength to propel the rock upwards.

It comes up so quickly, almost weightless in his hand that he overbalances, then scrambles back gracelessly, the rock still embraced as it literally explodes from the mire. He could not have imagined that it was so light; it must be hollow inside. Prepared for an enormous effort he has instead found collaboration underneath.

He lies on the ground embracing the rock. It covers him from waist to neck, side to side, a weight under which a man could expire except that it could not possibly weigh more than fifteen pounds. Hollow inside, he judges. Running his palms once again up and down the surfaces he judges that they cannot be more than an inch or two thick, a synthetic substance of some sort, inside the rock, emptiness. He might be

35

able to crack it with a blow, then core the rock like a fruit. But he has no curiosity about what is inside.

His curiosity has ended at the moment that the rock exploded upwards. Sensuous in its mystery, it has already lost some of its attractiveness for him; Folsom finds that he cannot, touching the surfaces, restore the sensations which orginally compelled him to yank it from the earth. With his fine, lucid commander's intelligence he wonders whether or not this might have been deliberate, whether the rock in some way is not, perhaps, *sentient,* was trapped in the earth *longing* to get out of it, was emitting strange thought rays which, operating on the pleasure principle, induced an onlooker to help it separate itself . . . no, he will not pursue this line of thought. There is simply no point in it and besides, strictly speaking, it is not entirely rational. Once you begin to believe that rocks on an alien world are alive it is only a matter of time and space until you get into other bizarre stuff like believing that the aliens are contriving a plot to destroy you or the other members of the crew are secretly working together to plot your overthrow. There is just no end to this kind of thinking once you let it overpower you and begin to seize control of your mind.

Folsom pivots to his knees, draws them up, works himself toward a standing position. The rock falls from him suddenly holding no further interest; he finds himself indeed scrambling from it. Suddenly he wants to put distance between himself and the rock, return to the encampment, see what they are doing with the native, whether they are extracting language from him, whether Nina might be interested, in the midst of her research, in nevertheless retiring once again to the floor of the forest . . . his thoughts, in short, are a welter of buzzing and flapping like busy insects circulating through the dome of his head, illumined by little shafts of desire. He wishes to get away from here. But as Folsom begins to move into the forest something as palpable as an enormous hand seems to touch him on the shoulder, yank him around and he turns, faces the rock once more, his eyes blinking, his hand rubbing the shoulder as if it had been injured.

The sensation of having been clouted is so real that Folsom finds himself looking for the piece of bark, the extraterrestrial object, the fleeing native that might have struck him . . . but the clearing is silent, there is no one there and after a moment Folsom understands that the blow must have been merely within his own consciousness; that is to say that it was some sneeze of the nerves, a convulsion of the central nervous system which yanked his attention around. Actually there is no one here at all. Smoke coils peacefully from a hut in the distance, little chirps of contentment seem to echo through the forest: this pastoral scene is overwhelming . . . and yet there was that enormous clout on the shoulder, as real as a fist, a call to attention as abrupt as anything which Folsom has ever incurred. His great commander's heart swells toward alertness; he cannot refuse this challenge. His attention is needed. Something must be understood. Perhaps it was his own subconscious which clouted him so although Folsom does not believe in deep convolutions of the psyche. He turns his attention toward the rock. The rock is the only fully unknown element in this scene, the call from the unconscious must somehow emanate from there. He moves toward the rock, crouches, peers, inspects it closely.

And yes, he sees what he should have seen before. Or, possibly, he sees what was not there before: there is no way of being sure. Perhaps it has suddenly manifested itself. Perhaps the rock is alive.

There is writing on it.

Raised off the surface in glowing little letters which seemed chiselled away as if with an inner fire are an intricate network of characters grouped together, separated by opened spaces as if they too were words. The characters seem to writhe as Folsom looks at them; like little animals they shudder away on the surfaces of the rock and then as he continues to stare at them, as if reproved, they cease their motion and lie flatly.

The symbols, of course, are in a language which Folsom cannot fathom. Never a linguist at best he finds himself stupefied by the circumstances in which he glimpsed this writing: there seems to be something menacing about it as if the rock had journeyed from a far place for no other reason than to taunt him with this message, almost as if the message itself in its indecipherable way contains an insult so deep, so scurrilous that it would have to be couched in a language which Folsom does not know if it were to be presented to him:

What does it mean? He stares at it and once again the letters begin to writhe; as if their secret of motility had been discovered and they therefore had nothing left to conceal, they do so almost defiantly, moving on the rock as if they were sheathes for creatures underneath which in their perilous footholds humped and relaxed their backs. Folsom shakes his head and moves toward the rock, raising his hand in a threatening way.

The letters smooth down.

Folsom looks at the rock, purses his lips, groans. His mission is clear and yet he does not know if he can bear it. His responsibility is absolute and yet he does not know if he can measure it. His obligation as commander is inflexible and yet he does not know if he believes in it.

Within Folsom's vast bosom, within his mighty heart the two beasts entwine and break apart, foaming, battling with one another. One of the beasts represents revulsion, disavowal, withdrawal, an unwillingness to pursue that which is not his direct concern: the other, a much older and stronger beast, calls itself Duty and is inflexibly opposed to that which it thinks of as the Enemy. But even though the Enemy is both younger and cowardly (it has existed only since the latch of the ship opened onto Folsom's Planet and this wretched but inevitable expedition began), it has its own advantages: low cunning, desperation, and the utter conviction that it is right. *Leave the rock alone!* the Enemy shrieks and hurls itself, little claws and talons flapping, across the honorable beast of Duty, there is that which you are not meant to know; do not concern yourself! don't you ever want to get away from this miserable place? and puts into Duty a bite so grave that Duty thunders with pain, reels, then unleashes a paralyzing blow to the Enemy which causes the Enemy itself to stagger away and quickly then, Duty is all over the hapless body of the Enemy, gnawing here, biting there, here a streak, there a clear, ringing slash to bring blood and the Enemy's cries turn into plaintive rumbles and at last whimpers as the strength flows from it and it lies, finally, on the desert of Folsom's interior, quite battered, beaten by God, Duty standing over it breathing heavily, looking at it with a fierce little expression of envy peeping from its demented eyes. At the heart, then, Duty can take no satisfaction. It knows that this has been a fixed struggle.

Grunting, cursing, moaning, pleading with himself, Folsom lurches over to the rock, picks it up. It vaults into the air almost weightless, no heft to it, no solidity, only its vast dimension obscuring his vision, making it difficult for him to see. Nevertheless, he must see, is that not correct? He has got to convey the rock back through the forest. Tears and sweat already obscuring his vision, a profound self-loathing in every pore, Folsom weaves and scuttles his way through the forest, stumbling from tree to tree, looking around the rock with the wild, tormented glances of a trapped animal to spot his way. He must take it back to the rest of them. He must show them what he has found. Then, at least, they will remember that he is the commander and that what he has brought to them could have been found by no one else. He wants to believe that. He wonders if the rock might be coated with an alien fungus which will affect his usual and highly dependable sources of strength.

VII

WORD FROM THE BUREAU: The days follow-
ing his discovery and conveyance of the rock pass to
Folsom as if in dull glaze, as if dropped into some
gelatinous substance. The normal passage of time,
something which Folsom has taken as much for
granted as his competence or the landscape of Folsom's Planet, seems to have been intefered with:
sometimes it expands, sometimes it dilates, it does not
move on its normal smooth track. Meanwhile Folsom
himself finds himself suffering from what might be
called a moderate dissociative reaction; he tends to
feel that he is apart from himself, looking upon himself, witness to rather than perpetrator of his acts.
He wonders dimly if this shows a failure of psychic
function; decides that it does not. It was made quite
clear to all of them when they entered the training
for the expedition that reactions of this sort might
occur. The long period of somnolence, the jarring
culture shock of emerging to a new world, the enormous responsibilities in which they would find themselves at once enmeshed . . . all of these, the Bureau
warned, might cause them to have a reorientation
of self, a temporary collapse of the self-image which
would result in difficulties of this sort. Folsom tries
all through this period to keep calm, to keep the
matter in perspective. Whatever else, it can be said
that the mission is moving forward. Everything will
be well. As commander, assuming that his subordinates
remain with their tasks, *his* only obligation is to keep
a firm hand on the proceedings, to inspire what in a

simpler time would be known of as Trust. He will do so. It is the least that could be asked of him.

Work with the native moves on smoothly. He is showing a vast range of knowledge, surprising in one coming from such a primitive culture and a high range of inquisitiveness, Stark reports. Not only does the alien want to know more details about the expedition and its members, the motives of the Federation, but he seems to have an insatiable thirst for specifics, the specific benefits, that is, that membership in the Federation will grant the members of Folsom's Planet. His demeanor is pleasant, his gross signs are well controlled: he evinces, Stark say, no haste whatsoever to return to his enclosure but indeed extends the sessions even longer than Nina or Stark or Closter are prepared to. His energy is inexhaustible. Folsom's own visit to the section in which the native is being worked upon confirms Stark's reports. To Folsom's queries he turns a pure, blank, trusting gaze of infinite sweetness and tact, to Folsom's brief inquiries the native responds in monosyllables. He will soon be ready for more complex dialogues, Stark assures Folsom, he will soon be ready to return to his village and function as intemediary for the races as they fuse . . . in the meantime it is best not to demand more of the native, perhaps, than the native can truly give. Folsom is convinced that the work is going well. He is able, in terms of the native's cooperation and intelligence, to measure for the first time the duration of the mission. Six months, perhaps seven at the utmost and he will be able to return home. That is bearable. He will bear it.

The rock remains where Folsom placed it upon his staggering return to the clearing some time back . . . nestling under a high tree, protected by gnarled, exposed roots and branches from the elements, sequestered in a pit of night so deep that only Folsom himself, knowing the location, can find it. The others would need his help to locate the rock, would have to beg his assistance if they wished to commence their research . . . Thus it is with some embarrassment that

Folsom must make an admission: none of them seem very interested in his discovery. In fact, since he brought it back, no one has made serious inquiries.

Oh, it is not as if his discovery was totally ignored. There was in fact a rather patronizing approval, much as if Folsom, being the only one of the four not equipped to deal with the native's education, was entitled to some discovery of his own, some little contribution to the mission and they had greeted it then with little explosions of interest, Nina, in fact, clapping her hands.

"Oh that's wonderful," Nina had said when Folsom staggered into the encampment with it. "Look what Hans has found, he's found a strange rock with cryptic writing on it!" and the others had nodded as if in agreement.

"We'll have to have a look at that all right," Stark had said. "It looks as if there are some *very important clues,*" and had run a finger across the raised writing slowly as if indulging Folsom, before pushing the rock away, suggesting that Folsom find a good place to put it so that very soon, when they had begun to establish communication with the community, they could get to it and start to unearth what clues might be locked into the strange writing.

Feeling somewhat manipulated Folsom had hefted his rock and taken it out of there: later, after he had placed it under the tree that feeling of insult had turned to one of heavy petulance. What right did they have to dismiss his discovery? and particularly after the trouble that he had gone to to bring it back to all of them. Who did they think they were? Somewhere in all of this was an obscure thought which buzzed in Folsom's brain like an insect; but he could not swat and capture it without destroying something valuable within his head so he let it be. But he would pursue it. That insect would come to rest and then he would see its nature.

In the meantime, the rock rests in its place underneath the tree and except for sullen walks to it now and then to make sure that it was all right and that

43

no member of the expedition or native was misappropriating what he had come to think of as his property, Folsom has put it very much out of his mind. He has as always his commander's duties; he has as well the problem of a puzzling message from the Bureau which has come in recently and which he still cannot fully interpret. Folsom would like to think that the miracle of instantaneous transmission which the Bureau has devised would be put to better use than the conveyance of material such as this. One of the things about technology which dismays him the most, as a matter of fact, are the uses to which it is put; there is nothing wrong, instrinsically, with the fact of technology but it must have more application than to the endless trivialization of the universe . . . ah, well, Folsom will not continue on this line. CONTINUE AS PREVIOUS, Bureau had noted, the symbols on the tape as luminescent as those on the rock and just as menacing, not less so because they were comprehensible, AND THEN CHANGE METHODS TO TRANSLITERATIVE.

What are they talking about? What can this possibly mean? Folsom, puzzled, had brought the roll to Stark just as soon as it had been passed through the decoder, but Stark had had little to contribute to his puzzlement. Stark's eyes had rolled back into his head in a peculiar and involuted fashion (Folsom was not sure that Stark and Closter were human; this might have been his basic difficulty with them).

He had said, "I don't know what to say. We've got our own problems in the field, of course. Field research that is to say. We're trying to establish a common lexicon."

"That doesn't help me," Folsom had said, and shown him the message again, thrusting it under Stark's eyes, rotating it before him. "You're the linguist here. You're supposed to be the communications expert. You tell me what they're talking about."

Stark shook his head. "I don't know," he said and then his features convulsed into something very close

44

to a leer. "Why bother me with this? Nina's a linguist too. Why don't you ask her."

"I thought I'd ask you," Folsom said sullenly. "I'm the commander here and I have a right to ask anyone that I want, don't I? Who are you to tell me who I can ask and who I can't ask something like this."

Stark shook his head, little lines of merriment concealed by the patterns of light of the fading sun, the breezes of the evening coming up to whip his face into a contrived solemnity.

"That's perfectly true," he said, "I don't mean to question your authority or anything of that nature at all but aren't you the one responsible for working with the Bureau? After all, you're the commander and we're the crew. It seems to me that it's completely your responsibility."

Well, Stark had been right of course. It *was* his responsibility, to decipher the messages from the Bureau and to deal with them in a fashion which would satisfy the policies and procedures of conquest while leaving the crew free to work on their own tasks of discovery. But that did not mean that Folsom felt himself any nearer a sense of discovery. He had decided to talk with Nina but she had been no more helpful than Stark, to say nothing of Closter with whom Folsom had lost all communication whatsoever.

"You know that I can't be bothered with that," she had said in a distracted fashion, wiping her hands across her forehead when he had summoned her from the enclosure. "I can't be bothered with that now. We're on the verge of approaching a full, cross-cultural index. Why worry about this anyway? Send them back a report; tell them that we're working it out in field study."

"But what does transliterative mean?" Folsom said, pointing with a heavy captain's forefinger to the word on the transcript of the communication, "what do they mean by this?"

"Everything is relative," Nina said. "It is all a question of context."

"That's good. Context is good, it's important. But what is the context here?"

"I'm afraid that I can't answer that for you," Nina said, "it's your problem. You're responsible for dealing with the Bureau, none of us are. We're only the crew," and had turned then, impatient with him, to return to the experiments. They had been running the alien through their network sixteen to twenty hours at a stretch. Folsom conld not comprehend their energy. How could they have devolved upon ignorance with such passion?

In that posture, Folsom thought, her frame tight, her body arched, her steps small but determined, in that posture it was hard to believe that Nina was his mate, the woman who had already consumated that relationship time and again with him on the floor of the planet, impossible to believe that this was indeed the woman who had gasped within his arms, convulsing slightly, churning out again and again the small motions of her passion: looking at her instead Folsom could feel an insufficiency which was akin to shame. He almost came after her to shriek about the rock and the strange writing on the rock . . . surely this would impress her, turn her clinical detachment to passion once again in the knowledge of what he, the captain, had risked to bring this back to her . . . but in the next moment Folsom's shame iced into harder particles because he recalled that he had already told her about it, told her several times in fact and that this had made no impression whatsoever. Whatever had been gasped out was in the past. She was totally committed to her work.

Folsom knew insufficiency then. He knew it as he had never before in his life: standing on the planet which was his own, commanding the mission which was wholly within his responsibility he had nevertheless, felt—and he had never felt this way before so it was utterly identifiable—absolutely impotent. It was unfair. It was unfair that they should have done this to him. They had sent him out to make contact with a stage three planet, administer the experiments

46

which would result in confluence and the beginning of cultural interlock and he had done all of this, going beyond his normal duties to bring back a rock which for all he knew might unlock further and more terrible tales of this world . . . and yet at no level did the very members of his expedition seem to pay him the proper credence; furthermore the Bureau was now sending him incomprehensible messages.

Inflamed by his rage, made terrible by this sudden thrust of insight, Folsom strode to the communications equipment and without hesitating activated the beam that would put him into contact with Bureau located inconceivably billions of miles away. His fingers shook over the console as he contemplated the audacity of this gesture which he was contemplating, the sheer inversion as this gesture contradicted all which he had been trained to accept: the infallibility of the Bureau, their irretrievable right to set a course of conduct, their implacability and finality. Thinking of this brought back memories to Folsom of the training process for the expedition and with them a dash of tears: he had been in control then. The crew had been under his direction, they had been assigned to him for obedience, and no one would possibly have defied his word. It was only when they came upon the accursed surface of this planet, began this mission, that the difficulties had begun. Can the aliens themselves, then, in a sense be blamed? Certainly it is a line of reasoning which Folsom would like to pursue at some crazier time. He had no difficulties with the command until they landed upon this planet, the only new element injected into the situation had been the natives, therefore they and they alone must bear culpability for what has happened now.

Well, Folsom will think about it. He knew from the moment that the alien had been brought into their encampment that something was terribly wrong with this situation. He should have forbidden Closter. That is what he should have done all right. He should have refused Closter permission to bring the alien back. WHAT DOES TRANSLITERATIVE MEAN?

he types with shaking fingers over the communicator grid. WHAT ARE YOU TALKING ABOUT?

The machine swallows the message, sends it shrieking through the starpaths. Aware as he is of the vastnesses of space, Folsom nevertheless thinks of it as a cubicle, a lightless cubicle, dense and damp around him through which messages between himself and Bureau pass like notes given one another by adolescents clamped into a small place. He knows that he should not think so; he knows that he should be overtaken by the starry dimensions, the awful, imponderable dimensions of the universe and the journeys which men trace out in that vastness but he cannot, try as he might, generate a sense of wonder. Taken from the training quarters of the Bureau to the hold of the ship, taken from the hold of the ship to unconsciousness and then to the floor of Folsom's Planet, Folsom thinks of his life, rather, as having been lived in a sequence of small rooms. For all the largeness of his mission, the potential of his search, it is clear to him that his motives would have been no more grandiose, his life no more different than if it had been lived in a three by five square. So even as the message goes tumbling end over end into the void controlled by the transmission, Folsom finds himself thinking of the compression rather than the dimensions of the situation, the perverse fact that for all the conceptualization of distances not only he but most people seem to live their lives within a series of small rooms. They will be able to bring that benefit to the natives of Folsom's Planet as well. Take them from barbarism, place them in an enclosure surrounded by machines.

Folsom crouched within himself, waits. At this moment he knows the message has appeared on the Bureau transmitter: he has no idea as to the actual dimensions of the reception room or its population but he conceives of a tired clerk sitting before the transcriber, slowly tearing off his communication, passing it onto another clerk, then to yet another, a whole hierarchy of damp, sweaty clerks sitting lined up by

48

the receptor machinery, taking in the messages from a thousand planets, twelve hundred, whatever number (it is never less than a thousand) are under exploration at the present time; all of the clerks would be dispirited and weary but still able, and during their free time which is given them by the Bureau ten minutes on the hour to gather in the small recreation room, they would exchange desultory gossip about the latest happenings on the planets: fragments of scatology, little hints as to the quirks of the various commanders. The clerks are not well compensated but they are the lifeline of the Bureau, this is made quite clear to them (and to the commanders as well; respect is to be paid them at all times) and they are entitled to take a certain amount of pride in their position. First line of defense and so on. Folsom, looking at the communicator, thinks of his clerk now breathing slowly through his open mouth, small vapors condensing within and without him while taking the message over in a fast limp to the next line of authority who has a worse limp and difficulties with his eyesight. This, however, makes no difference. Folsom will have to wait.

He does so. There is nothing else to do. His presence is not needed with the native, not needed in the village, not even needed in the great ship which is self-sustaining, remote-controlled right through the airlocks when it is unoccupied. Folsom must admit this: he has no function. It is not the first time in his life that he has had this thought but never has it struck him so cruelly: there must be another way in which duties could be distributed. Why should the commander who is responsible for every facet of the voyage, why should the commander lose all his authority, become a subordinate figure precisely at the point when he should be most in control? It was unfair, Folsom thinks, for him to be placed upon this planet which bears his name (his own name!) only so that he could be a witness to the efforts of the crew. Something will have to be done about this. He will have to file a complaint. He definitely will have to make a report about this. Why has no one ever done it before?

The communicator begins to chatter. The sound is noisome, shocking, so neatly has Folsom been locked into the temple of his consciousness, his sullen retrospection. Paper begins to move out of the belt, the keys hammering and Folsom looks at it fascinated as if it might bear some revelation which would absolutely speak to his condition. TRANSLITERATIVE MEANS WERE DISCUSSED THROUGHOUT THE TRAINING PROCEDURE. IS SOMETHING SERIOUSLY WRONG WITH YOU?

Folsom looks at this. He scratches his head, thinking of the sallow clerk, energized by his task of reproof, typing this out. For the first time it occurs to Folsom that he might have misjudged the Bureau. It is not benign at all; to the contrary it seems to be irretrievably hostile. I DON'T KNOW WHAT YOU ARE TALKING ABOUT, he types out with a shaking forefinger. TRANSLITERATION WAS NEVER EXPLAINED.

The communicator swallows this up. Appalled, Folsom watches it disappear through the void. Appalled, through filmed eyes, he watches the communicator seem to become translucent before him. Appalled he waits for the response.

There is no way in which he can explain the feeling which he has, hard even to phrase it, but waiting, waiting there Folsom feels moving within him the clear, dark intimation that an important part of his life is ending and another, no less important, but far more painful, is about to begin.

Simply stated, he has never comprehended the language. He sees that now.

And it is too late to learn.

VIII

FIRST CONTACT: Later that night as I lay on the earth, looking at the spare and grainy inner surfaces of the tent, my eyes seeking through them as if instinctively for some patch of the night, there was a rustling outside and the sound of footsteps. Instinctively, with my great commander's reflexes, I reached for the weapon at my side to protect myself from the invader but when the curtains parted it was Stark, Closter and Nina who were standing there. Nina framed between the two, looking solemn, her eyes becoming round as she saw the weapon . . . and with a feeling of revulsion I put the weapon at my side, half rolled onto it as if to conceal it and said:

"What is it?"

Their eyes were still on my hip concealing the weapon. They could not believe, obviously, they could not believe that I might have shot them. This proves along with everything else that they have no comprehension of the duties of the captain, the great isolation in which he must walk, his powerful and dangerous heart which expands, as it were, to defend himself and his crew against the beasts of night. "What is it?" I said, discouraging their stares. "What do you want?"

"The alien will speak to us now," Closter said, looking at me in an appraising fashion. "We have established communication."

"Full communication," Stark said. He seemed to move subtly behind Closter, his eyes busy, active, concerned with the granules on the canvas. "We thought that we would report this to you." He paused,

51

shook his head, then stepped in front of Closter. "After all," he said, after taking a breath, "You're the commander. We thought that you would like to know."

"You would have shot us," Nina said. "You would have killed us."

"You didn't say anything," I said. "How would I know who it was? I had to protect myself. You've got to take precautions."

"What precautions? Who else would have come in here at this time?"

"You never know," I said. My embarrassment was acute, yet well-controlled. I would not yield any of it to them. Looking at her in the twinkling, sudden light of Folsom's Planet which, just as the Bureau had predicted, revolves around its sun exactly as does the Earth, rendering it to the same cycle, making it an even more desirable third stage planet, I could see that any relationship between us was now truly finished. Mating procedures or none she despised me. "You just cannot tell," I insisted, "you have got to be prepared for all eventualities."

"You would have to be insane," Nina said, "to want to kill us," and moved away from there, her face a disappearing bulb in the darkness, moving away from me in a kind of complex frieze; her face was a series of still-lifes which finally passed away from here, taking illumination with it until only Stark, Closter and I were there to confront one another in the midst of burlap. Stark's voice was shaking uncharacteristically as he said, "Would you like to see him?"

"See who?"

"The native," Closter said. "We've established full communication . . ."

"I know," I said. "You said that already. But what is there to see?"

"You might have some questions to ask?" Stark said.

"But I don't," I said. "I have no questions to ask. This is not my responsibility, you know that. The responsibility for achieving communication is your own; how many times have you said that?"

Nina's departure had put me in an even fouler

temper, that and the indistinguishability of Stark and Closter. Not only their dialogue but their very characters were interchangeable; it might have been not two men standing there but one who had doubled himself. There seemed to be something profound about this fact but I could not locate it.

"Is that what you came in here for?" I said, "to tell me meaningless things like that?" I rolled over, felt the prod of weapon under hip. "I'm not interested," I said, "I'm not interested in your filthy little experiments. As far as I'm concerned it's out of my control."

"Don't you want to see him?" Stark said. "We thought that you would . . ."

"No," I said, "no, I do not," but even as I was protesting in this way something strange was happening; I was beginning to move. Limbs flailed in the old and accustomed ways, the consciousness moved at cross-angles and then I was standing, swaying, looking down at Stark and Closter who—and I should have commented on this a long time before—are considerably shorter than I am. As, of course, they should be. The commander is the tallest of the crew; this is mandated for psychological factors.

"All right," I said, "all right, I'll have a look at him."

"That's good," Closter said. "We thought that it would be best if you did. After all, when he returns to the encampment, matters should go very rapidly. We thought that you should check on him first."

"Very kind of you," I said. My limbs felt vaguely disconnected, there was a disoriented sense of weaving as I stood between them; then I moved slowly toward the tent flap. "I'm sure you've done wonderful work."

"Oh indeed," Stark said, "it's surprising how well you can do with them, what you can dig out if you simply approach it from the right direction. Do you know something we've found? They're *eager* to communicate; they were just shy and frightened. According to their mythos we're the vengeance gods come to wreak retribution upon them. They couldn't understand why, after our initial appearance we simply didn't destroy them."

"That's fascinating," I said. "Why do they believe in vengeance gods?" Actually, this was merely a means of making conversation. I had no concern with the aliens; the only question, staggering at the ridges of the mind, was what had happened to Nina? Where had she gone, why had she turned on me in this way? I would not have thought that I could have generated the feelings of impotence and dismay which possessed me. In the darkness, the floor of the forest seemed to be filled with small, dangerous animals snapping away at my heels. I walked carefully, lifting my feet away from the source of the menace, glimpsing the faces of Stark and Closter in little off-flashes from the half-moon. The atmosphere was extremely earthlike but I was not lulled for an instant: I knew that we were on an irretrievably dangerous and alien world, billions of years from home and that there would be little assistance from the Bureau in the completion of our extremely dangerous mission.

"That seems to be part of their mythos," Closter was saying. "Remember? I discussed that with you before. The fact that the myths seem to be strangely monotheistic, reflecting a level of cultural integration which they don't seem to possess in any of their other folkways. The vengeance gods are historical forerunners of the monotheistic tradition of course."

"Of course," I said, "of course, you're absolutely right, there," and Stark took a firm grip on my shoulder, impelled me then toward the left and through the flaps of the enclosure in which the alien sat before a low fire, looking at me from shrouded eyes, a strange look of—perhaps this is anthropomorphism—cunning in his eyes as they blinked once, twice, seeming to absorb me with the light of their gaze. Looking at him I could feel for the first time that sense of humility which the Bureau instructed us we would feel when dealing with alien races, alien contact . . . a sense of our insignificance in the void, the marvel of the processes which had resulted in this sudden, powerful connection with the source of our history. What can only be called a sense of wonder overcame me as I stared at the alien and he, in turn, stared at me. Closter gave a palpable chuckle to the rear as I looked at the alien and then seemed to disappear behind the burlap, leaving Stark, the alien and myself grouped together in a tight and uncomfortable position.

"He is in full communication," Stark said, "you may talk to him." To the alien he said, "This man is named Hans Folsom. He is the commander of this expedition."

The alien nodded gravely. Little folds of flesh under his throat moved, a fine spray of sweat seemed to spread a halo around him. "I am pleased to greet you, Hans Folsom," it said. "My name is Ezekiel."

The tone was surprisingly pleasant, surprisingly lifelike. If I had expected that this native, given speech, would talk in a different timbre, if I had thought that the sheer alienness of his condition would cause him to speak in tongue and tones incomprehensible I was wrong . . . for his voice had the spare flatness of the very agent who had converted him to speech: he sounded, in fact, chillingly like Stark himself. The possession of language had not changed his aspect, then, so much as it had merely flattened it: declension, possibly, is the word. He had fallen away from the position of an impenetrable and noble savage to the accessibility and rather noxious familiarity of Stark himself . . . who stood there grinning.

"Isn't that remarkable?" he said to me. "Ask him anything you want."

"What do you want?" I said. The alien looked at me with a solemn, considerate gaze, his aspect shifting now to one of sympathy. He seemed to be trying to commune. "What do you want?" I asked again.

"I want to learn. That is why I came here. I came to learn from you."

"Do your people want to learn?"

The native gave a distinct shrug. He was not quite as old, I saw now, as I had originally taken him to be.

55

Disease or dilapidation would, of course, be quite common with primitive folk of this sort; the team had done a remarkable job in dewarting, shaving, cleansing. He appeared to be a fairly vigorous male in the bloom of years.

"I do not know if they want to learn," he said. "I only know that *I* want to learn. That is why I am here."

The emphasis was well-placed, the timbre quite lifelike. It was obvious that the team indeed had done a striking job. "Who calls you Ezekiel?" I said. "Is that your name for yourself or is that the name you have been given?"

"He has been given that name," Stark said. "His own appears to be unpronounceable."

"Given by who?"

"By us of course."

"Why?"

"Actually," Stark said, "actually it wasn't my idea, it was Closter's. It was kind of silly but I let him have his way. After all, he *did* do so much of the work and his own specialties are mythological . . ."

"Still don't know why," I said. I had the illusion that in the darkness the alien and I were exchanging a look of understanding, that we had been welded together, collaborators against Stark's babbling idiocy. This was an illusion, of course, the alien and I having little enough in common, but a comforting one. I felt quite abandoned at that moment. "Why don't you tell me . . ."

"Ezekiel was one of the minor prophets in the Old Testament," Stark said. "He wrote about various visions given him by angels of the Lord."

"Old Testament," the alien said rather thickly. His pronunciation was impeccable. *"Old Testament."*

"Old Testament?" I said.

"One of the books of the old Bible," Stark said. He paused. "I admit it was a rather silly idea."

"I don't see the point or purpose."

"Well," Stark said clearing his throat, "the point is that to us this native, Ezekiel, might take a position

56

of prophet to his kind. And of course he sees us as gods. Isn't that so, Ezekiel?"

"Yes," the alien said agreeably. "You are the gods. You are the Thunder Gods of creation; you have come to save us and to bring us universal peace."

"Who's been teaching him this stuff?" I said. "Who's been talking about Thunder Gods?"

Stark gave a little cough. "I *told* you I rather thought it was silly. I had nothing to do with it at all. It was Closter's idea. He thought that it might be amusing."

"We're not Thunder Gods," I said to the alien. "We come representing the Galactic Federation."

"I know that," Ezekiel said. "I know about the Galactic Federation. I was explained to all of that. But I prefer to call you Thunder Gods."

"You see?" Stark said, "he doesn't mind it at all. He likes it. We wouldn't do anything against his will."

"We are not gods," I said again. "We represent the Federation. We come from a world many billions of miles from here in peace and to help you but we are men just like yourselves."

"What are billions?" Ezekiel said.

"Do you see?" Stark said. Even in the dark I could imagine the smugness on his face, just from the way in which his voice came forth, the compression of the cheekbones, the tilt of arrogance. "He conceptualizes only within certain limits and, of course, we must work within them. What is the difference anyway what he thinks of us? Communication has been established! Ask him any questions you wish."

"But this is not right," I said slowly. It would be difficult for me to seat the basis of my anger, the slow, patient necessity I felt to make this point. "It is not right to teach him that we are gods."

"Thunder Gods."

"Of *any* stripe. How can we train them, how can we involve them in the Federation if they look upon us as gods? Right away the whole notion of eventual equality has been destroyed. Don't you see that?"

Stark said, "I see everything, Captain. I had never heard him use the formal term before and there was something jarring about it, I felt myself instinctively bracing. "Why don't you take care of the command facilities and leave the matter of linguistics and social interaction to us. Do you have any questions to ask Ezekiel before we send him back to the village?"

"You are in conflict," Ezekiel said flatly. "The two gods are in dispute. Gods are fighting among themselves; the heavens thus are shaking. This is one of the signs of the approaching end, when even the gods will fight among themselves."

"Is this what you have taught him?" I said. "Is this what you have been spending your time doing?"

"I told you, Captain, that the matter might best be left . . ."

"This is disgraceful," I said, "I will have to make a full report on this. It is not supportable . . ."

"I'm afraid that this is getting us nowhere, Captain. I'm afraid that we are only wasting our time here. If you have nothing more to say, I am going to give Ezekiel final instructions and send him back to his people so that the process of assimilation may begin. It was only fear which held his people back from us, not hostility. They will be eager to cooperate and the sooner Ezekiel returns the sooner the process will begin."

"Yes," Ezekiel said, "my people are eager to worship the Thunder Gods now that we will know the language."

"Insupportable," I said again. I stumbled against a mud wall of the enclosure in my rage, staggered into little springing shoots of vegetation which seemed to have been implanted within the wall, brushed at my face teasingly, tauntingly.

"You are filling up this alien with cheap mysticism, cheap nonsense and it will not redound to our credit. You know what the Bureau will say!" I screamed and reeled through an abcess of wall, into the cool and shrieking night. There, feeling the breezes waft against my face, I felt calmer, felt that I had made a spectacle of myself and that perhaps I should return to Stark, apologize for my outburst, but in the next moment when Stark had come from the enclosure to rail at me I felt that impulse ebb and with its ebbing, strength returned. He stood there, the alien at shoulder-height beside him and shouted imprecations, imprecations at me, the Captain, and the rage was within me again. "You fool," I said, "don't you realize that this is insurbordination."

"You have no right to interfere with the acculturation process. You have no right to question our methods and particularly not in front of Ezekiel; we are trying to reinforce training and now you are . . ."

"I don't care" I said. Powerful in my rage, I felt the clarity of design. "You are confined to quarters, Stark! I have the authority to do this . . ."

He came up, touched me with the lightest and most tentative of touches which acted only to compound the rage. "Captain," he said with a genuine and quiet curiosity, "Captain, are you mad?"

"Send the alien back to his people!" I said, "send him now!" and wrenched myself from that grasp, turned, spun, cracked Stark across the face, feeling my fingers dig past flesh to the bone, the arching, defiant, mutinous bone of him and with a little shriek he fell away. I turned then toward the alien, my impulse powerful: I think that I might have struck him too (and this as a violation of the code of conduct would have been serious; under no circumstances are we authorized to impose our will physically upon unaffiliated races) but I was saved by Ezekiel's own alertness: with a strange little cry he dodged my intention and turned then, came up and past me, and then was gone into the forest. Dark blob against darker blobs, he passed into invisibility and I stood there over the heaving and weeping Stark, a sense of catastrophe working through at all levels, a sense that perhaps I had overreached myself but for all of that I felt pleased, quite pleased—and I am not denying the rising pride—because I had at last asserted myself. I had shown them that liberties could not be taken. I had shown them that there were limits beyond which the commander in his rightful post could not be pushed without terrible retaliation. Thinking so, I stood there in the forest, hearing, with an unnatural perception, the sounds of Ezekiel as he ran back toward his settlement, listening to Stark's little moans and snuffles and then insight burst upon me like a great, rotten fruit, like the sun exploding to reveal the corrupt filaments within; I understood then what the Bureau might have meant, what *transliterative* meant, and the thought was enchanting; it was as if the key to a new language, the language, say, upon the rock, had opened up to me and that I could understand it; in that new world of possibility things which I had never before understood broke open one after the other—I might have been Ezekiel himself absorbing information out of the coding devices—and there is no saying how long I might have stayed there, Folsom lost in his new world of contemplation and connection, had not Nina emerged from the brush where she might have been for a long time and come up to me deliberately and deliberately she reached forward and slapped me a ringing blow on the face much like the one I had administered to Stark who, reciprocally, gave an *ah!* of approval on the ground.

"You fool," she said, "you've really gone and fucked things up this time."

And looking at her delicate face crumpling indelicately now in rage, I began to see that she was right.

ASSUMING CONTROL: With Stark confined to his quarters, with the reassertion of his control over the mission, Folsom moves past that moment of doubt and indecision, decides that even with all the difficulties which have been brought upon him by the crew he feels somewhat better. He never should have let the mission out of his hands, that was all. He should have remained close to the procedures in the beginning.

Now, in the flickering, wasted light of the crude lamps lining the clearing, Folsom addresses the other two, Nina and Closter, in what he has declared to be a formal session. Stark's moans and contortions from the tent in which he has been bound are somewhat disconcerting but Stark is helpless and Folsom decides to ignore him. The other two are sullen, defiant, dangerous themselves but they are essentially contained and Folsom knows that they will abide by the compacts. They must: he is the commander, he is the only one with requisite knowledge of how to fire up the mighty machines, seal up the locks of the great ship; without him they will never return to Earth. So they stand quietly as Folsom speaks to them, keeping his voice low and controlled. Fine streaks in the dark invisibly marking the place where Nina had struck him seem to glow within Folsom's skin; in that mesh of pain he senses a beacon which may guide them to the source of that pain, his disgrace . . . but he will ignore that. Nina too is simply now an enemy; she is one to be dealt with. "We are going to cease attempts to communicate with the aliens at once," Folsom says, "and we are going to make preparations to debark from this planet. I am putting in the request to the Bureau after this meeting to allow us to debark."

This incites no comment. Perhaps they have nothing to say. Of course there is the matter of his prior actions being extremely upsetting but Folsom cannot allow personalities to enter into the matter. This is not the commander's concern. As far as he is concerned anyway, the incident is closed.

"I have my reasons for this," he says, "upon which I do not care to go into detail at the present time. There is no reason for me to do so: the regulations on this point are quite specific. The decision as to the point of conclusion of the expedition resides solely within the commander. It is his to make. It is completely between the commander and his own set of judgments. And in the commander's opinion this mission must be terminated at once."

There is more silence. Closter and Nina look at Folsom impassively; if he were equipped with a paranoid frame of reference he might think that they were in some obscure way out to get him. As it is he could not be less concerned: they *cannot* get him. No one can. He is the commander; he is invulnerable.

A rich scream from Stark pierces the stillness. It moves up and down the scale in vibrating fashion, holding at the top for a while, then sliding down to a profound baritone wavering with pain. Folsom clasps his hands, listens to it without apparent emotion. Inside he is suffering of course but he will not show this. Nor is there any point in demonstrating his emotion; he must preserve a steely mask. Closter twitches, his knees shake, he seems at the point of standing and bolting to his distressed mate.

"Don't think of it," Folsom says coldly, "just stay there. He is perfectly well, he is not in pain and he is responsible for this."

Nina says, "Do you have anything else to tell us?" She clasps her hands in unconscious mimicry of Folsom's, inclines her head. The half-moon slashes light across her cheekbones; truly she is most attractive. She has never been more attractive to Folsom than she is at this moment. Not that this bears any relevance of course.

"Why yes," he says, "I have a great deal more to tell you but I'll do so in my own time in my own way. I want to know now why you went across expressed procedure and told the alien about the Bible."

"The what?" Closter says, "what are you talking about?"

"You know perfectly well what I'm talking about," Folsom says with superb calm, monitoring his breathing, his pulse, the dull regularity of his life-support processes with dispassion while he meets Closter's luminescent eyes. "You named him Ezekiel as is in the Old Testament. In so doing you talked to him about the Old Testament, about its secrets and its history. That is expressly forbidden. Our traditions, our mythos are private and not to be shared with any stage three race."

"You're crazy," Nina says, "you've got to be insane."

"Ah," Folsom says and leans forward over the improvised lectern which he has hastily assembled from chopped down twigs and little branches, propped against one another in the mud, "ah, you say that I am crazy but that is because you realize the seriousness of the situation now. You know the consequences of your act and the terrible penalties . . ."

"You are crazy," Nina says again. She stands, moving from the half-crouch with which she has assimilated this information. "I won't listen to this any more."

"You had better listen," Folsom says with his newfound calm. Stark shrieks again; it is only obligato to his purpose, he ignores it. "You had better listen to what I'm saying; we could all be in the most serious trouble because of your stupid error and you cannot walk away from it."

"The man is suffering," Closter says, gesturing toward the enclosure. "At least let us minister to him."

"In due course," I say. "I am the commander and

63

will decide when you may treat him and when you may not. I intend to keep a much stronger hold on your behavior than in the past; I do believe that this is the only way to solve the problem. Only way to solve the problem," I repeat judiciously and stand, tower over them, impressing them with my height and power as well I might since I am the commander and physically far superior to any of them. I should have taken this line a long time ago; we would not have gotten into such difficulties. "Is that understood?" I say.

They look at me unspeaking. I can see the one sliding crosswise look which they exchange, a look which is supposed to be below the level of my apperception and which communicates, of course, a whole battery of message. It does not bother me. Another rich scream from Stark opens up the darkness into little ghostly shimmers of light. He is bound up quite tightly. "One more thing," I say. They look at me sullenly. "There is to be no more contact with the natives."

"Why?" Nina says.

"Because I order it. We are going to debark just as soon as we can get the approval through; in the meantime we are to stay away from them. Further contact would be extremely dangerous."

"We can't avoid contact," Closter says quietly. "Ezekiel has been sent to the village to instruct them and to bring a delegation who similarly want to be socialized. They will be coming here."

"Then they will be turned away. Forcibly if necessary."

"I don't understand why," Nina says. "I don't see why it has to be this way," and then as if having made some complex series of considerations, while some intricate balancing wheel of the psyche turns inside her, she sits quietly, says nothing whatsoever. I can feel her implacable hostility pouring from her like heat and I can feel Closter's as well, but hostile reaction of course is the inevitable concurrent of strong command and it does not bother me. Nothing bothers me; in truth I feel very much in control of myself. "All right," I say, "I am going to ask you to return separately. In the future there will be no contact between you unless I am present. I am invoking martial law."

Closter stands and says, "Can I take care of him now?" motioning in Stark's direction.

"I suppose so."

"That's very kind of you," he says. He lumbers off into the darkness. I watch him go, shrewdly, measuring. Nina coughs and then stands.

"Wait a minute," I say.

"What?"

"I said, wait a minute."

She holds in position. My power over them is astonishing; my prerogatives absolute, it is again dismaying to think that I could have done this a long time ago and saved the situation. But at least I have done it now. I look at her and in the darkness she assumes another form, something for which I have no words but which has an alternate reality. She could be an alien. Perhaps I am thinking of her as an alien. "I want you to go with me," I say, "I want you to look at something."

"Look at what?"

"You'll see," I say. I move over to her, touch her hand, lead her. She comes into my grasp easily, the collaboration of her body a mockery of the older collaboration I have known. Putting my hand on her shoulder blades I can feel through the resilience that it is over: Nina and I will never have sex again. Mating or not, the ancient codes of command overweigh the more modern ones of connection: I cannot, in the new position that I have assumed, show any softness. But for all the feeling of detachment and control there is sadness as well. Our copulation was good. It was life-sustaining. How was I to have known that it was not only that but the seat of my weakness as well?

Like dancers we move through the forest toward the place where I have hidden the rock. I feel an inexplicable excitement rising, knowing that I am going to show it to her. Caution will not hold me back nor will collaboration: I want her to see it. The secret which has been buzzing and flapping in my head hammers now at the ridges of the skull, causing a feeling of dislocation. What will the rock reveal? What will her appraisal of it tell me?

"Faster," I say. I am pulling her. "Come faster."

"You're hurting me," she says. She gasps, stumbles through the foliage but I increase the pressure on her. "You're crazy," she says again. "I think you're mad."

"I'm not mad," I say, "I just want some answers." Now I am in the little glade where I placed the rock.

"There," I say and point to the rock.

She looks at me. I can see her fact distinctly in this close aperture, her eyes are stunned, she seems absolutely beyond speech. "What do you want of me?" she says then, "what is this for?"

"That," I say, holding my finger steadily, unwaveringly on the rock, "that is what I want from you. I want you to tell me what that is."

"You're hurting me. You're lying on my leg."

"Yes," I say, "yes of course." An odd courtesy and tenderness fills me, I roll away from her, whisk myself to my feet, lean over, scraping off little fragments of dirt from her and then extend my hands to lift her to her feet. She comes up quickly against me in a dancer's motion, I feel the cool slant of her fingers within my hand. An odd sense of communion fills me; I am touched by her. "That," I say motioning to the rock once again, "I want you to tell me what that is."

She looks at it with interest. In the little spokes of light from the moon the writing is distinct, the background has a brownish hue I had never noticed before. It is almost as if the rock were a living thing and it was sprouting little vegetation in its hidden place. "Tell me what that means," I say to her.

She looks at it still. I can tell that her desire to be dispassionate, to remove herself from me is being throttled by something else, something which could be described as scientific detachment. Although she hates herself for it, the rock interests her. I stand back so that she can get a better look. It is quiet and dense with foliage here in the forest. It occurs to me that I could force myself upon her here and no one would ever know. For that matter, who would protect her? Of course I would not even consider doing this. "I don't understand it," I say.

"Where did you find this?"

"I found it in a clearing near the village."

"And you brought it back here yourself?"

"Of course I did. Who was going to bring it back for me?"

"What did you do that for?" Nina says. She crouches carefully, moistens a fingertip with her tongue, wipes it across the surfaces of the rock. Do I imagine this or do the letters seem to respond with a tentative little glow, seeming to squirm over the surfaces? She wipes her hands on the cloth over her knees, stands. "This is fascinating," she says. "I don't understand it."

"I thought that you might."

"I don't understand any of it. You mean you found this yourself and brought it back here on your own? Why didn't you tell us about this at once?"

"I'm telling you now," I say. "Isn't that enough?"

"But you should have told us immediately. I don't think that this is a native object. It seems to be an artifact of some kind."

"I didn't have the chance to tell any of you. You were so absorbed with the native."

"Is that why you made us release the native? Is that why you've put Stark under arrest? Because you didn't want us to deal with the native, you wanted us to look at this?"

I feel almost abashed. As always, with that concentrated insight of hers, she has come close on to the truth. "Maybe," I said. "That wasn't all of it. There are even more important things but I thought that, yes, you could have taken a look at this . . ."

"Then why didn't you ask us?" she says.

The question sets me back. Indeed, why did I not simply call their attention to this? "I wanted you to be finished with your studies," I say, and then add rather vaguely, "but you wouldn't be. Not within a normal span of time. You just went on and on and you weren't getting anywhere."

"You're insane. You know that you're insane, aren't you aware of that? You've got to know that you're crazy."

"I'm afraid that you understand nothing. There are certain obligations which as commander of the expedition I have to serve; I couldn't expect, of course, that you would be concerned with them."

"Where did you say you found this?"

"I found it in a clearing near the village. I could show you the exact spot, I suppose, if you wanted. Can you understand it?"

"No," she says, standing abruptly, "I can't understand any of it. I'd need to spend hours and hours with it, I can't tell a thing just by looking. Also, we'd have to work together."

"Who would have to work together?"

"The full team of course. We work in tandem. You can't expect that any of us could do the job alone."

"No," I say, "you are not going to work together. That's clear. That's quite definite. The team is broken up and your research is suspended."

"Then I'm afraid," she says, "that I'll be able to tell you nothing."

"What does the writing mean? What does it have to do with us?"

"You're insane," she says again. "You've gone quite mad. You can't really be serious about this, can you?" She approaches me, stands inches from me, her mouth accusatory, her hard, high cheekbones radiating their own subtle message. "Is it this that has driven you insane?" she says, gesturing back over her shoulder to the rock. "Could that be the explanation for this?"

Suddenly I am overtaken by desire. It hits me with a clout between the shoulder blades, much as I had been stricken in that moment before I had seen the rock. It is just as if a giant hand had come from the heavens to smite me, an idea of reference quite common with megalomaniac fantasies as I understand it but then again I am hardly an introspective type. The blow knocks me forward, sends me to my knees and in the same gesture I have extended my arms, seized her wrists, dragged her down to the ground facing me.

She crumples in astonishment, leans against me and says, "What are you doing now?"

"What do you think I'm doing now?"

"I won't," she says, trying to claw free, "damn it, I won't do that with you!"

"You've got to," I say, "it's the compact." Although lust has already made my voice indistinct, I am muttering syllables rather than words, parched little phrases rather than full sentences, and lying against her, pressing her into the earth, it is with the great throb of desire that I speak and I force myself down and against her.

"Come on," I say. "Come on, you have no right to deprive me. I've been patient. I've waited; I haven't forced you to do anything but now I demand my rights." I draw my hands up her arms, quivering. "My rights," I say, my voice almost breaking, and try to gather her into me. She fights against me kicking and squealing, using my strength against myself to throw me off and I roll over on the ground, stab into a tree and then lie there quietly. Gasping I come to my knees, remove and point my weapon at her. "Don't force me," I say, "don't force me to use this."

She shakes her head. Oblong on oblong in the darkness, convolutions of the body working at cross-purposes. "You wouldn't. You wouldn't do anything like that."

"Yes I would. I would have to."

"You couldn't. You couldn't force me . . ."

"I can't put up with it any more," I say, "and it's not my fault. Now I have my rights too. What I did to Stark I can do to you. Do you want to be imprisoned? Do you want me to make a full report to the Bureau on insubordination? We're not going to be on Folsom's Planet forever, you know. You could spend a long, long time under confinement."

Movements cease. "You are mad," she says, "you are really mad."

"No I'm not. I'm simply assuming control."

"But I don't care. I don't care any more. I'll fuck you. Come here."

"Good."

"Just put that weapon away."

"I already have."

"I'll even study your rock for you. I'll do anything you wish. Anything! Just get me out of here."

"Oh I will," I say, "we'll be leaving soon. It won't be long now until the instructions come through."

"It better not be."

"Everything will be fine," I say. Little swatches and patches of song once again begin to brush against the seat of memory; I find myself humming as I cavort slowly toward her, the ground swelling on foothold like an animal, seeming to rise to greet the little prongs of my feet as I move toward her, the air itself delicate, warm, caressing, never have I felt the atmosphere of Folsom's Planet to be such a palpable thing . . . and then my lust, guiding me home, takes me close, takes me against her, I swim into her arms, piscine, I rub my scales and fins against her, insert my claws in her arms, her own unnecessary coverings fall away, we fall away together and there at the bottom of the world we copulate, I am plunging in and out of her, thickly; demanding renewal from the engines of her body, I find a collaborative rhythm within her, work on it. draw it out, beat it through my blood and brain . . . and as I rise to come shrieking my eyes are focussed on the rock, the hieroglyphics gleaming in the crazy moon and at the summit I almost think that I can read it but later on, collapsed across her like a dead fish in the bottom of a boat, I understand that I can not.

DELEGATION: On the next morning or perhaps a little while after that, Folsom's sense of time being somewhat jarred and disturbed by accelerating events, a delegation of natives, led by the Elder who has been trained, appears at the edges of the clearing, then comes through in solemn, single file. The Elder, leading, sweeps the terrain, obviously looking for the others but I am, per my own instructions, the sole occupant of the grove. Stark remains in confinement, Closter, sulking, is with him; Nina has returned from her adventure with Folsom in the wood to her own enclosure and may be sleeping although then again she may not. Folsom finds himself uninterested; his sexual juices drained, his concern with Nina is at a low ebb. One could say that his emotions approach true detachment.

Ezekiel and his followers—Folsom makes it five of them—stroll through the glade in rather stately fashion, Ezekiel in lead, the others looking at Folsom with shy, hesitant glances which seem to have an underlay of lust (is his mind unbalanced? one will have to see). At a point of five feet removed Ezekiel stops, waves the others to halt and gestures in a friendly way at Folsom. There are three mature males, two mature females in the group, dressed in their simple, humble barbarian garb. Only Ezekiel seems to have altered his costume. He wears a cloak of rather regal cast although stains from top to bottom undercut its impressiveness. He gestures toward Folsom.

"They have come to learn," he says.

"That is good."

"Are the instructors here?"

"They are not available," Folsom says impassively. He shows a commander's firmness. "They are involved in other duties at this time."

Ezekiel thinks about this, drawing fingers across his handsome chin. He appears quite humanoid: not only has this socialization process given him language, it seems to have provided a definite and accessible personality. "I would like to see the others," he says to Folsom, "so that all may be helped to learn. It is important that we wish to learn." His syntax is off subtly but this only allows his meaning to shine through the more clearly. "May we see the others?" he asks again.

"I'm afraid that's impossible," Folsom says. He reaches down a clawlike hand, fondles his genitals. The gesture is half-unconscious, a small itch has framed his attention and he is not even aware, strictly speaking, of what he has been doing until the glare of Ezekiel, narrowing in on that point, functions in reproof. Folsom feels a slight blush moving into the abcesses of his cheekbones, he slaps his hand down to his side. "I can't arrange that," he repeats, "it can't be done."

The natives look down at the ground with abashed expressions. In their bestial way, they are rather attractive, Folsom notices. He has never really been close enough to any of the females up until this point to make that judgment, now he can see that even in their simple agrarian, pretechnologized, barbaric state these females are not yet unknown to the purposes of a rather sophisticated sexuality. He finds that one of them is looking at the ground and giggling, her little shoulders moving subtly and it is all that he can do to restrain himself from breaking out in giggles as well. Really, he can see the humor of it. Only a fool could not see the humor. It is a fine day, a wonderful day, and he no longer has to worry about Stark or Closter; he will never have to worry about them again.

"I'm afraid it just can't be done," Folsom continues cheerfully, "they're busy right now. Besides," he adds gently addressing Ezekiel directly, "I'm afraid that there will be no more communication with you. We're going to be leaving you soon."

"Leaving?"

"Yes," Folsom says. He gestures up toward the sky, a luminous, porcelain blue, inverted above them, seeming to hang in fingerholds over the tops of the trees. "All the way up into the sky and out again. Our business here is at an end."

"The Thunder Gods? Are going to go up into the sky?"

"We're not Thunder Gods," Folsom says gently. His patience seems limitless this morning; there seems almost no end to his ability to deal with the situation quietly, constructively, happily. Boundless as his patience is, even more equable seems his mood. At this moment it is as if nothing could hurt him. "We're visitors from a far different world, a world far away from yours, but we are men just like you, not gods."

Ezekiel looks at him with a hanging expression. Perhaps the native is not very bright or perhaps there have been gaps in the training administered by the faithless Stark and Closter. "But I don't understand," Ezekiel says, "you are gods."

"Afraid not," Folsom says, "afraid not at all. We're just men, very much like yourselves, and our mission here is completed."

Ezekiel shrugs and turns to the group. He says something in the strange gutturals of the language, the fluid, melodic sounds making Folsom feel suddenly melancholy. They are far removed from him; he cannot understand them. Granted the essentials of his mood: his optimism, good cheer, the feeling that he has passed a threshold of doubt and moved into an utter sense of control . . . still, it is sad to witness in this rapid conversation of theirs that much of what they communicate is truly unavailable to him. Stark and Closter would not have been so puzzled. Doubt-

73

less, they had made inroads to the language. Still, there is little sense in worrying about this. Stark and Closter are not near the situation.

Ezekiel's message seems to spread ripples of agitation through the others. They confer, grouping their heads together, little anthropomorphically observed expressions of dismay flickering across their faces. Folsom stands and watches them impassively. They have lost the capacity to move him. One of the females touches Ezekiel by a sleeve, moves him in closely, whispers something to him urgently. Ezekiel inclines his head, then raises it to Folsom. "When are you going to leave?" he says.

"That is not certain yet. Soon. As soon as we have obtained permission."

"Permission? Gods do not need permission for our acts."

"We are not gods. I have already explained that to you. We are creatures much as yourself, simply on a different level of technology."

"What is technology?"

"That is very hard to explain," Folsom says, "I cannot tell you about machinery quickly. I can only tell you that we, just as you, must listen to and confer with others before we perform certain acts."

"Machinery I understand," Ezekiel says. "Machinery they have explained to me." He looks over Folsom's shoulder, his eyes becoming abstracted as they stare into the distance. "Do you mean that we will be unable to search out the others?"

"That is correct."

"They wanted me to return with others who wished to learn. I have brought these others."

"I am sorry," Folsom says. Firm insistence seems to be the best way to deal with the situation; he feels an awkwardness that he would not have predicted. The aliens have put him slightly on the defensive. "I am the leader of this expedition and it is my decision that you are not to see the others."

"What is the leader?"

"That is hard to say also. I cannot explain it to you."

"So what are we supposed to do?" Ezekiel says. "Return? Leave? The Thunder Gods would not like that, I was told. The Thunder Gods wish us to stay."

"I'm sorry," Folsom says. His defensiveness has increased; his voice seems to be shaking. Agitation is nothing that he can betray for Ezekiel and the others and he suppresses it with a swallow, points out into the forest. "You must leave," he says again. "You must leave now."

Ezekiel leans toward the group again, confers. Their syllables are disjointed and arcane; Folsom can make no sense of them but their mood seems to be very sober. "That is bad," Ezekiel says finally, the others backing away. "They are very disappointed. I am very disappointed. This is not what was expected."

"It cannot be changed."

"Will you talk to the others? Will you tell them that we were here?"

"I will do that."

"Perhaps they will want us to come again. Perhaps they will come to the settlement. At the settlement then, we will wait for them."

"Waiting will do no good," Folsom says, "They will not be there. They will be leaving shortly." He does not know why he is so insistent upon this point. He cannot quite understand it. The important thing is that the natives are leaving, that he, Folsom, has assumed full control. Why must he argue with them, deny them hope with every other quality? He is not quite sure. He backs away from them a pace, gestures. "Leave now," he says.

"Very well," Ezekiel says. "It is very saddening." He runs his hands up and down his clothing, seems to be trying to adjust it into a tighter and more attractive fit but after a few such spasmodic motions he backpedals, moves to the center of the group, gestures again. They nod, then turn and trudge off into the forest. In no more than twenty paces Folsom has already lost them; they have been trapped from vision by the trees. For a little while he hears their

75

footsteps and then he hears nothing at all, hangs at the center of the forest solitarily, feeling abandoned. He wonders if he did the right thing.

Oddly enough, regret claws at him. Perhaps he should not have dismissed the aliens. Perhaps he should have differently approached the matter, offered them confidences, refreshments, some display of friendship before he turned them away. The females were not unattractive—he feels the perversity stirring within his mighty commander's loins as he once again thinks of the females, disgraceful, perhaps, but they *did* tantalize him—and he might have won their confidence, might have set up a situation in which, at some later time, he could have fornicated with them if he had desired. He has no right to reject the possibility out of hand, they might be trapped on this planet forever, they might find themselves unable to debark and it would be a handy thing if there were a number of females around who took him to be one of the Thunder Gods; it would certainly ease his commander's solitude, his commander's duties. But he knows, even thinking this, that it would have been wrong and that he has done the right thing here. He has not taken advantage of their superstition, of their simple, agrarian condition; he has functioned with them, in fact, very much as a Thunder God might . . . with dispassion, pride and detachment. Remember that, Folsom thinks. Whatever else can be said you treated them better than the others. You did not take advantage of them.

The thought gives him little comfort but then he really did not expect that it would. He is merely trying to sustain himself against the clamorous feelings of guilt which he knows might otherwise assault him. Guilt has nothing to do with the situation; he really has done the best that he could have, granted the failure of cooperation from the Bureau, the murderous instincts of the crew, but he knows, of course, exactly how much appreciation he would get for that quality. No one cares, that is all. The Bureau with its insane and escalating demands, the loathsome crew, the intolerable Nina . . . all of them sucking away from the vigorous and articulate Folsom the very core of his personality, making a mockery of his contribution.

Well, he will think of that no more, Folsom decides. He will not wallow in self-pity: he can put that behind him, be really dispassionate. The situation with the mutinous crew has been resolved, the natives have been dispersed back to the village, only the Bureau itself remains and he will deal with that right now. He walks vigorously back toward the communications shack, striding with a vigorous stride, thrusting his chest out, delighting in the evidence he is showing of good physical condition. Despite the fact that he is thirty-two years old, Folsom thinks, no one would suspect him of losing the slightest edge of combat readiness; he is as prime a physical specimen as he was when he enlisted in the Bureau's expeditionary division at the age of twenty-one. Better in fact; in the flower of his maturity he is a better man than he was then. His thoughts are shrewder, his insights keener, his sexual performance infinitely more studied and regularized, his gross, motor signs functioning within a tight and ever tightening limit. No one would ever accuse Hans Folsom of not being in the flower of physical condition, he thinks. No one would say that Folsom is not a good example of what a commander should be.

Striding toward the communications shack, he whisks past the tent in which Stark and Closter are, the burlap discreetly closed as if against invaders or winds. He decides that he will not look in there, not check upon their present activities. Why should he? All that he will see is what he remembers from the last time and he has no desire to become involved with either of them again. Stark will be hunched over in his bonds muttering, straining his wrists helplessly against the binding rope, whispering confidences to Closter. Closter will be patiently feeding him or giving him advice, reminding him that the bonds can neither be loosened nor slackened without physical damage being done to him. The two of them will be perched over one another; Stark's condition was like that of birds tapping at a feed tray. They will both remain there past any point of dignity and if Folsom were to look in they would give him long, glum looks mingled with revulsion which would surely depress the sensitive Folsom . . . so why bother? Why bother indeed? He strides rapidly past the enclosure and into the communications area where he sees that a message from the Bureau has already been delivered, lies gleaming dangling in the rollers. It must have been there all night. There is no saying how long that message has been there. Staring at it, Folsom has a sense of horror: could he really have been so preoccupied with his own difficulties that he would let something like this go, embarrass himself once again? Well, obviously. That is exactly what has happened. He must stop this, Folsom decides and wills himself to do so. Now that he has matters once again under control, lapses like this are unpardonable.

He leans over, reads the message. It seems to be a paraphrase, rather an extension of previous communications. TRANSLITERATIVE PROCESSES ARE CONTINUING, Bureau has pointed out, FULL DISLOCATION IS NEAR.

Folsom stares at the message for a while. He is sure that it makes a consummate kind of sense, the same sense that prior communications have made but then again something may be wrong with his brain or the transmission machinery. Looking at it in any event gives him the same dull pang as he had witnessing the first except that this pang is more extended and nearer the surfaces of his heart, a feeling of great gaps opening in tissue, of blood oozing out. He is not as greatly physically preserved as he thought he was if words on paper can do this to him. FULL DISLOCATION IS NEAR. What is full dislocation? And why is it near?

His fingers, beginning to shake in the old, accustomed fashion, Folsom leans forward and hits the keys. He does so with great concentration, tongue tucked near his palate, teeth poised against one another, great, intelligent eyes staring luminescent at the keyboard. Only the dishevelled aspect of his cap, the hairs drifting over his forehead, would give clue to his agitation but no one, of course, is there to observe this. SEEK PERMISSION TO TERMINATE EXPEDITION, Folsom types out, the message whisking through the aether (to his vision) like smoke. UNEXPLAINED FACTORS NOW PREDOMINATE.

Let them consider that a while, he thinks. Let them mull over the import of his communique, those dull clerks at the Bureau until at last they will reach a confusion to duplicate his own; past that confusion will come submission. They will grant him permission to leave.

He really should have put through this request before, Folsom thinks vaguely. After all, he had represented to the others that he had received permission for termination from the Bureau and to his mind at the time that he had told them that, the idea of requesting and receiving permission had seemed almost synonymous. They had all blurred together. Thinking about it was just the same as having it done, that had been the way that he had looked at the situation but maybe, he thinks, that was not quite right. Something is wrong. He hadn't asked for termination. He was only doing it now. Something seems to have happened to his sense of time; midway through this adventure it has become muddled, even fractured.

Be that as it may. Folsom sits before the communicator and waits for the response to come through. Of course they will permit them to debark. There is no alternative to this. Is not Bureau, ultimately, sensible? Of course it is. Besides, the precariousness of the situation here would be obvious to anyone not a fool and although he has had his quarrels with the clerks at headquarters, Folsom has always retained a strong, underlying faith in their efficiency and good sense. He puts his life and trust in institutions. He has been doing it for thirty-two years and so far none of them has failed him, Bureau will not either.

He sits and he waits and as he waits he thinks but what Folsom thinks about is best not recounted here as the sum effect of his life is bested not in thoughts but in vigorous action . . . and action is what the Bureau has sought for him.

XI

FUNNEL: Lying in the ship in the days before the descent, in the pit of sleep, Folsom had had a dream and in that dream he had been screaming in space. Suspended without the protective hulk of the ship, bare to the ether itself, he had hung in the small, gravitational field which the ship projected and traveling alongside it, a mote in the endless universe, he had screamed and screamed for a thousand years while the ship had turned itself around slowly and begun its cautious, graceful descent toward the surface of the planet.

The dream had been so vivid that Folsom, even though he had known with some open layer of the mind that it was only hallucinative, had felt himself possessed with the real conviction that he was subsisting in space, alternately freezing and being devoured by flame as the ship closed its gap of space and time. He had hovered in the field like an insect, shouting and battering at the hull, pleading with his companions to save him but of course all of his companions were sleeping so there was no help in that direction. There was no help in any direction at all. Folsom knew that he would die out there.

Amazingly and despite the lack of atmosphere he did not. He lived without breathing, circled without motion, screamed without sound. Oddly, despite the obvious difficulty of his circumstances he seemed capable of surviving. Space came in upon him in its nakedness and its power but space did not wrest from Folsom the gestures of his mortality. It was, in that sense, a dream which had not only a powerful sense of conviction but an ironic undercurrent. It seemed to be not only a terrible and tragic way to suffer through the months of unconscious but a wry comment upon his condition. For what was he if not suspended in space, what was he if not in the sleep without mortality? Folsom, not a reflective type, could, upon emerging from this (for every element of the dream was accessible to him, he could reach with a retrospective finger through to the unconscious and rummage with it) see the justice to it.

It was as if some great dislocative murmur of the ship, perhaps as it hit an obstruction in space, had jolted him into the corridors of this dream for he remembered distinctly that he had not slid into unconsciousness with it but had, indeed, found it under that layer. Something must have happened to them in the voyage but what it could be Folsom did not have the slightest idea. He never discussed his dream with the others—they simply did not talk about things like this—but from certain furtive aspects of their expressions in the first hours of shared awakeness, when together they had prepared the ship for its descent, he had had the feeling that so it had been with all of them, that something had happened to send all of them into space screaming and now they would never talk about it.

This was a shame. Folsom wished they had. He might have learned something, checking all of this through. Of course it is all too late, now. Most of it.

XII

TACTICS OF CONQUEST: As I waited for the response to come in from the Bureau I rummaged around the shack incuriously, the actions desultory, merely seeking a way to fill time until the response which would liberate us from the planet would come but in my search I came across some of the preliminary reports which Stark had filed and I found them so interesting that I quickly became absorbed in them. Stark was an excellent writer, an excellent sociologist: it was a pity that he was such a fool, that he had so little control over his ability to deal with people in a pleasant, cooperative manner . . . but this had nothing to do with his reports which were concise and extremely helpful. It made me wish, in a way, that I had gotten to know him better.

Folsom's Planet, according to Stark's best deductions, was uniformly in an agrarian or (in the isolated sectors) preagrarian stage. The age of the civilization which we had observed could not have been more than five thousand years and internal evidence provided indicated that it was quite a typical society; that Folsom's Planet was composed of two to three hundred tribes living throughout the thinly populated corridors of the planet, these tribes only in the most marginal communication with each other. Occasionally nomads or madmen exiled from their cultures would wander a far distance but by definition nomads or madmen had little to communicate, were of low credibility. The tribes existed virtually independently of one another. Stark speculated that they were all within similar levels of agrarian achievement;

none of them had entered the state of technology. If they had, there would have been inferences of cross-cultural seeding. That was how he put it. "Cross-cultural seeding."

The tribes probably averaged a thousand or two in population. The one with which we were dealing was probably typical in that regard; the natives were shy but Stark calculated from evidence of land use and landscaping that they composed a population of approximately fifteen hundred. More than two thousand in a tribe or village, Stark had speculated, would probably be unwieldy in the simple hierarchical social units which had been devised and there probably would have been a splitting off of one part of the tribe against the next, a war leading to disbanding. But the hierarchical system and crude methods of birth control were functional to keep the tribes within controllable limits. Stark felt that actually the societies were extremely functional and well-integrated; granted that Folsom's Planet would be left alone, that there would be no induction of technology from the outside, functional elements, primitive myths and anti-technological superstition might contrive to keep them in this state of moderate barbarism for several thousand more years. Eventually there would be population overrun, eventually one tribe or another, after a war might stumble into technology, but Stark saw little indication of change deduced from the external evidence in several thousand years. In truth, he considered the present social mix to be extremely stable.

The hierarchical system was similarly functional; the aliens were a patriarchy, leadership descending through inheritance of no more than three or four male lines within a given tribe. The leaders worked under the divine right scheme of course, but according to Stark, they were held in check by the mythos which held that their function was only to work the will of the minor gods and one did not, eternal life being at issue, go around offending those gods. It was a neatly functional system. Stark's handwriting

84

broke into spirals of pleasure when it made these comments. Above all, it worked: something which for a sociologist must have been engaging. So little else did.

The only interesting element according to Stark was the monotheism. Tribes at this level of agrarian or preagrarian development tended to have a whole host of gods for various duties, gods for various aspects of their lives and yet these people—who of course did have a galaxy of gods which in their language were known as the "lesser"—did believe in a strong, unifying superstructive force observing all of their activities, controlling some of them and this one was indeed known as "God" as opposed to "the gods," an important distinction of which the natives themselves were quite aware. Stark could not understand this. It seemed out of kilter to the culture; it indicated a level of sophistication which was present in no other facet. Yet the observance of, the belief in, this God was absolute.

It hinted, Stark speculated in his rather disjointed sociologist's handwriting, it hinted of perhaps an earlier technological civilization which had disappeared without a trace of its machinery or accomplishments but which had managed to leave behind as legacy this religious vision, the only characteristic of the more sophisticated culture to survive. Monotheism in one or another of its various forms was an inevitable concurrent of a technological society; it did not exist independent of some technology . . . except in the case of Folsom's Planet. Stark admitted to some puzzlement. So did I.

Not a reflective or contemplative man, however, I put aside the matter of Stark's conundrum and considered my own situation. Research had its virtues of course and it was interesting to see in Stark's writings the output of a competent, thoughtful sociologist; it also was highly illuminating in its insights into his rather tedious but accessibly obsessive personality, good material to transmit to the Bureau at some later date . . . but I had my own situation to consider.

Tossing aside his notes, leaving them in a rather disorderly pile atop the abcess from which I had taken them, I stalked through the spaces of the communications shack to ponder my position.

In some ways it was good and in other ways it was bad. This is one of the characteristics, it must be said, that I have noted about life itself: sometimes good, sometimes bad, but always, at least in my case, dotted with a certain low consistency which means that I am never at a loss for the best way to deal with a situation, having seen it before in some other way in the past. Life is merely a matter of successfully recalling past experiences for referent. (This is why I have a commander's facility I might note.) The good things about the situation were that I had assumed total control, that I had stopped allowing the crew and the natives to push me around and was once again where I belonged on top of the situation, the other good part was that I had communicated to the Bureau the urgency of my request for the termination of mission and it would only be a matter of time now until the Bureau responded with permission. It would be unprecedented for a commander in the field to be balked. This is part of the clear policies and procedures of the Bureau as established through hundreds of years of interstellar scouting for the Federation: that the field commander is supreme.

These were the good parts of my situation, that and the fact that my own mood had improved so enormously once I had seized control. Truly I felt like myself again. But there were bad aspects as well and I had to confront them straight-on: whisking little clusters of dust from untended parts of the shack, clearing away a little space in the alcoves where Stark and Closter had heaped the residue of their scholasticism, vigorously stroking certain random itches which smote my genitals much as random and uncoordinated reflex activities might overtake one in the coils of paraplegia, I was ready to confront those as well.

For one thing the mission had clearly failed. Contact with the stage three civilization, their amalgamation into the great Galactic Federation, the successful continuance of permission to seed the stars with the fruits of our civilization . . . that had been aborted. Our relations with the natives, our establishment of contact had hit against a wall of failure and there was no way that this could be denied: in our essential purposes we had been frustrated. There were reasons for this of course and the reasons when communicated to the Bureau would fully explain the reasons behind this and would release me from any culpability for the failure: they would, in fact, when explained, probably render me fit for commendation . . . still, from the Bureau's point of view the aborting of the mission had to be considered in an unfavorable light and they could hardly be pleased with the turn that events had taken: at this moment clerks and superiors were undoubtedly shouting at one another, copies of my request dangling from the hands of the clerks as they made little explicatory thrusts with their palms; the faces of the superiors would be livid with rage as the clerks tried to make them understand that according to the manual they had no right to do other than to grant the permission to debark . . . oh, it was very unpleasant at the Bureau now for sure, I was grateful thinking of this not to be a part of it. Eventually all would come right, they could not deny the strength, the grace, the sheer courage of my gesture, but that would be later. After our return. After we had been in flight for three years of unconsciousness by which time Bureau would have had another one of its devastating transitions of personnel anyway and we would have to start the explanations from the beginning. That was the trouble. You could never quite get it right.

XIII

RECOVERED AS IF IN A DREAM: After the message from the Bureau, Folsom, still disbelieving, feeling his body beginning to recoil in the accustomed shock always felt when there was a sudden overload, left the shack quickly, trying, for some reason, to be as unobtrusive as he could, to leave as little evidence as was possible of his having been there. He straightened out Stark's material, returned it exactly to the position in which it had been originally, whisked off the little stains and dust motes which his presence had induced, even rolled out the used paper in the device so that he would leave no evidence of his having been there. A fantastic neatness, in short, overcame him and it is difficult to say exactly why Folsom would react in this fashion because to the best of his knowledge, no one would ever be in the communications shack again to make deductions of any sort.

Having done this, trying to maintain an elaborate casualness, Folsom strode from the shack. In his hand he clutches the sheet on which the Bureau's final message is printed, it curls into his palm, nestles there like an animal, the letters glowing. They seem to have the same sensation of upraised surfaces and fiery messages that his rock did but he does not need, unlike the rock, to look at them in verification; he knows that they will not change. His breath is even, regular, his gross motor signs continue to be controlled and well-regulated. He would give to no external appearances whatsoever the appearance of a man in deep shock.

No. The commander must be controlled at all times; there is no excuse, regardless of the circumstances, to let slip the mask of his efficacy. He will not betray feeling. If any alien had moved out from the village to spy upon him, which is the kind of thing that they might do (despite their apparent fear of him), the filthy little buggers, that alien will see nothing. No one will see anything. He is Hans Folsom, the commander. He has fulfilled the obligations of command. He is in perfect control of himself.

Nevertheless, despite these thoughts, despite frantic little monologues which he gives to himself consisting of approval for his appearance, his demeanor, his wonderful self-control—Folsom finds that his control finally breaks. It might be the fifth tree he passes or then again the sixth; it might be in mid-stride or at the conclusion of a step when he lands wrong, twists his ankle on a stone, goes plummeting to the ground at one of the very places where he and Nina have copulated; it might be some accumulation of all these factors, but finally his wonderful commander's self-control breaks and Folsom finds himself weeping helplessly into the foliage, little knives of vegetation prodding into his eyes as he draws a cupped palm to his face, hears as if he were someone else, his sobs beginning conversion into racking, vomitous moans. It is not fair, that is all. They do not understand him. They have never paid him the proper credence, they have never from the first taken him seriously and now, at last, his wonderful old commander's heart has been torn apart and he cannot understand why it has happened or whether he will be able to live with this new condition. How could they have done this to him? Truly it is not fair.

And lying there, sobbing in the vegetation, the response from headquarters curled into his pocket, the past begins to filter through Folsom in little bits and pieces, first slowly, then more rapidly like a great torrent of water pressing from some weakening point of a dam or then again possibly the image he is striving for is that of a cerebral hemorrhage, a colorful cerebral hemorrhage opening up layer after layer of capillaries in the skull, flooding the brain in fluid, the brain slowly inverting in its case, the past pouring from the brain like blood and Folsom finds himself in a clear, lighted place, a glade that must be where he has just finished fucking Nina, and now he is standing, his face distended with feeling, little pockets of emotion bulging in his face, his cheeks bloated and he looks at her down on the floor of the forest, his love, his necessity, his receptable, broken like an hourglass below his feet, her mouth staring up at him quavering and Folsom says, "You lousy bitch, you lousy bitch, how could you have done this to me?"

She looks up at him saying nothing. Her face is bruised, her eyes blotched with small marks where he has struck her, her body collapsed to vulnerability beneath his, her breasts devastated with the small and terrible marks he has left upon her and yet she will say nothing at all. Stubborn, that is all it is, the quality of stubbornness but there is nothing divine about it, quite the opposite, there is scatology and the diabolic in her stubbornesss, her refusal to break under him.

"You bitch," Folsom says again, "everything could have been fine, everything could have worked out perfectly and then you had to start dealing with them. You and the others." His handsome face twitches in an ugly and tormented expression. He bends, searches his discarded clothing for the weapon which has been there all the time in preparation for a moment such as this.

"It could have been wonderful," Folsom says, stroking the cool surfaces of the barrel, so unlike and yet so reminiscent of the shape of her body underneath his grasp just a few moments ago, "We could have taken care of everything, it could have been a simple project and then out of here but no, no, you had to get scientific, you had to start negotiating, you had to *teach* them things and now you won't even tell me about the writing on the rock. It's a plot, that's all it is, a plot which you've worked up to humiliate me but I'm too smart for this. I'm too smart for any of you; I'm the commander of this expedition and that means that I don't have to put up with any of this shit. I can assert control anytime I want to; you just think I'm stupid because I don't have a scientific specialty or don't know how to talk to those filthy disgusting little natives but that doesn't mean a goddamned thing. Not a goddamned thing," he repeats and pauses, listening to the sound of his heartbeat, rocketing away in his chest like the explosive drive of the engines on takeoff. Really, Folsom knows, he should get hold of himself. Everything that he is saying is absolutely true but she is in no position to take any of it and besides he should be restrained. He should control himself. He should keep a lid on his emotions; that after all is the commander's responsibility.

Still, it is hard to do so considering everything that he has been through. He levels the weapon again at her, fixing her in the sights and realizes that his finger is shaking, sweating, straining against the trigger. Would he really shoot her? No this is impossible, it is inconceivable that he would so lose control of himself and yet it is with a wrench of effort that he forces that palpitating finger away from the trigger, drops the gun to his side. Little drops of sweat gather and fall into his eyes like rain. "Don't you have anything to say?" he says then, "don't you have anything at all you want to *say?*" She lies there, still in broken position, but he takes her impassivity for stubbornness and not for the pain that it might really be. "You had better say something," he says, and raises the weapon again. "I can't go on this way. You've got to talk."

"You're crazy," she says then in a low, parched voice, drawing breath on every syllable. *You're cray zee.* "What's wrong with you? Get away from me."

"You don't like it, do you?" Folsom says vaguely. He does not quite know what he is referring to but it has the ring of absolutism. "You don't like it at all."

"Get away," she says again. She flexes her thighs, a fine droplet of semen seems to wink from the orifice, drip like a tear on the ground and it is this, like a finger at the back of his brain, tearing his brain across, that must send Folsom over the ledge of uncertainty and into action; action is after all what he craves, he is a man of action pure and simple . . . he would not have gotten into any of his current difficulties if he had from the beginning followed the path of activity. Was that not right?—of course it was right. Folsom lifts the gun and as rage sings through him much as tunes and lyrics had done much earlier, producing the same burble now in the esophagus he levels the gun and . . .

He takes the gun and he . . .

He points the gun all the way into her and he . . .

Surely he recollects this perfectly; what Folsom does, the righteous rage moving through him like blood, is to take the gun and pointing it down at the shrieking woman he manages, finally, to . . .

Well, something has happened to his mind. Folsom, strolling through the little tunnels and burrows of the past, hunched sobbing in the vegetation, is yet unable to bring this clearly to mind. It has something to do with what he did to the woman with the gun, that is clear, but try as he might he cannot quite push aside the stony obstacles, see what has happened. It is as if the rock which he had discovered were leaning in the cave of his consciousness, blocking off his vision of the scene and struggle as he might, he cannot twist the rock aside so that he can see. Very well. So be it. It will come back to him later, Folsom is quite sure of that and if it does not, well, that part is all right too. There is a reason for everything. The world makes sense. If he was meant to remember what had happened, he would have, in due time he will. Of course he will. He twitches a little on the ground, sweat ballooning to fill up the eaves of his clothing. He feels a little nervous and a little distracted but basically he supposes he feels well. Continue to probe. Probe the past. He fondles the sheet of paper containing the response from the Bureau. Look at it again? No. He is not quite ready to do that either. Everything in its place. When there is a time there will be a season, a reason for every place under Heaven.

After the woman. After what had happened on the floor of the forest. He had moved away from her, leaving her there, walking toward the enclosure where Stark and Closter had been. To see them. To see what they were doing, that they were well. Even though he had had his disagreements with them, he was still the commander and responsible for their health and well being. That was a commander's obligation. Insubordinate, defiant, dangerous as they were, they were still in his charge and Folsom accepted that responsibility. He wanted them to be well. He wanted them to continue to remain in good health and spirits so that they could be transported back to Earth, taken to the Bureau, subject to departmental hearing on their insubordination, taken out and shot.

Surrounding the enclosure where the two of them were, a nest of insects swarmed out, attacked Folsom, biting him fiercely on the cheeks, energetic, vicious little pellets darting through and around him. He had never before been aware of insects in this forest; he had been taken by surprise. The reports had been clear: there were no identifiable animals on this planet, nevertheless, there were the insects. Folsom had no idea where they could have come from, nevertheless there they were and with little wheezes of fury he wiped them from his face, flinging them in small, gnarled handfuls to the ground and then, as he stalked toward the enclosure, the insight came clear: *they* had done this to him. Stark and Closter had turned the insects upon him. All of the time that they had been in confinement they had been sniggering and collaborating working out their wretched plan to strike back at him and now, in the aftermath of the attack they were probably whinnying with laughter underneath the burlap, laughing at his condition.

Well, he did not have to take that. He could put up with a good deal in his capacity as commander, it was his *duty* to suffer the excesses of the crew but there were limits; he had passed them. Once again Folsom felt the weapon leap into his hand, once again he felt the power surging through the metal as he plunged wildly toward the enclosure where the two villains skulked after having committed their terrible deed.

Outside the enclosure they were waiting for him. He had not seen the villains in the off-angle of light, the sudden gloom (perhaps a projection of his mood) which had fallen upon the shelf of the forest, but as he came close upon the enclosure, waving his weapon bravely, daring them to come and confront him, he saw that the villains had indeed emerged, were standing there, Stark still in his chains, Closter holding him protectively, looking at Folsom.

Folsom at once deduced the seriousness of the situation. Against his explicit instructions Closter had been released; this should not have been. But it was even more serious than that: having released the insects (which still seemed to buzz and chatter busily around his head although not with the abandon of a few moments before) they had perpetrated a direct attack against the person and position of their commander, Hans Folsom, leader of the expedition, discoverer of Folsom's Planet.

Now it was not the person under seige which bothered Folsom; he was a mild and unassuming man, a man utterly without vanity and indeed with a certain becoming *je ne sais quoi* of modesty which ideally suited his even-tempered application of the commander's role, no, it was not personal abuse which bothered Folsom for he had been prepared from the very outset to take abuse from this mutinous lot . . . but the attack upon the position of the commander, the mighty and terrible office which he held, this is what Folsom resisted and what he could not bear.

For in insulting the command function the villains were not only undermining the mission, they were undermining, eviscerating, detonating the very nature of command itself which went back through untold generations, through the history of the great Federation and the Bureau which administered it, which stretched in a great, grey unbroken line back to those primitive days when the teams had just begun, when the Federation had been a struggling union of two or three planets deemed to fight for common ends to save the universe from barbarism . . . but even then the Federation and the Bureau had been under the dictates of what had been the truism which had led them to greatness: that command was absolute, that the office was to be respected, and that the fate of the commander was inextricably bound with the mission and with the great agencies which administered it.

They had fought for the primacy of command. They had fought for it on the glaring, red sands of Mars, they had fought in the green and swampy jungles of Venus, in the louse-filled pit of Jupiter they had struggled with gasses and the beasts for a captain's word. On Saturn's rings hundreds of men had died to uphold the word of the commander and his right to do as he saw fit, on the cold, dead plains of Neptune that message had been known again and again for which twelve thousand had been doomed. And so this message had been taken out of the barracks of the solar system and onto the stars themselves— that from command radiated the great power, the force, the control which would make over the universe in man's image but only if it were respected. To dishonor command was to dishonor mankind itself, to undercut the commander was to crush man, to defy the captain then was to fling disrepute upon the millions who had denied themselves so that quality could be preserved, could be exalted.

It had been the command function on Sirius the Dog Star, had been command again in the Rigel System where the invaders and monstrous beings had been crushed, had held true on Algol VII where the great war of the frog men had resulted in their rout and in the glorious victory of the Federation even at the cost of several hundred thousand brave troops . . . and now, on Folsom's Planet, the villains Stark and Closter heedless of all history, mocking the past, mocking the quick and the dead, the brave and the fallen, the followers and the crusaders alike had chosen to defy Folsom by freeing themselves from arrest and sending a mass of insects to buzz around his head. Folsom could not put up with it. There was no reason why he should take it. If he did he would open the door by implication to the rout of the Federation and if there was one thing which Folsom was not going to do it would be to dishonor the Federation in any way at all. For he had dedicated his life to doing nothing that would bring discredit upon the Federation and upon that in which its spirit dwelt, the Bureau, even though the Bureau was certainly acting very strangely these days and was doing little to help him in his desperate and awful mission.

"I've got to do it," Folsom said and saying this levelled his weapon; in the next moment the two knaves had scattered before the bore of it, looking for positions of safety within the enclosure but Folsom knew all of their crude and desperate trickeries and was not going to be cheated of his just and terrible revenge. "You cannot do this to me, I don't mind it personally but the Federation can't stand it!" Folsom cried and saying no more levelled the giant weapon and cut them down in their . . .

He cut them down . . .

He hurt them very badly . . .

The blood was leaping; their bodies seemed to explode . . .

Explode rising into the air, the deadly fountains, the . . .

Folsom took the weapon and aiming it pointed . . .

He tried to take the weapon and . . .

But he can take it no further; once again the walls are sealed up, the great rock has filled the crevice and Folsom, try as he must to break through the seal, cannot do so. He does not remember exactly what happened. It had something to do with what he did to the villains of course, the same thing, probably, he had done to the female who had opposed him but he is not too good on the specifics of the thing. Perhaps it would be best not to think about it any more. This kind of retrospection can only lead to difficulty and in any event Folsom must put the past behind him. The past does not matter; the mission has been wretched, this is true, but it does not have to continue within that state of wretchedness if he will only put it behind him and concentrate upon the future. The future looks considerably brighter; it is of a different aspect than the past; while the past seems to be a closed tunnel of gloom, the future is bright and yellowing before him if only he can break through this sudden enclosure of thought to come out the other end to see it. He will have to see it whole. Bureau was all wrong to do what they have done but, Folsom thinks, to hell with the Bureau also. What do they matter? Ultimately they must defer to the decisions of the field commander; the word of the field commander is supreme and if they do not like what he is doing, then they can take it and, well, they can stuff it. This is what they can do. *Stuff it*. Folsom finds that he feels considerably better. Having wrenched these words, this attitude out of himself it is as if some enormous weight has rolled away and he is fully restored to the man that he was.

And indeed it is true, it is true: weight has been displaced. It has been taken away, the enormous rock cleaved to the walls has rolled to the side and in the cave of consciousness Folsom can see the clear light filtering. He sees not only the future in this sudden input of light but, if he wished, he could see the past as well. It is there now if he only wanted to look.

He does not want to look. Having resolved to put it behind him, he can no longer be concerned. The past happened to some other man in a different stage of life; he is always changing, now, despite all of his difficulties, he is still growing. He has moved beyond it.

Folsom's limbs twitch, scramble on the ground. He puts his palms flat to the floor of the forest, arches his body, gathers his feet underneath him. Slowly, he rises, wavering slightly in the shade of the trees, adjusting his eyes to this arching gloom revealed from a different perspective. Little shadows cleave in and out of his damp eyes, shattering his vision. Then it is pieced together slowly and he can see.

Slowly, as if with the weight of all the great responsibilities of command itself—which he will never, never be able to leave—Folsom shuffles off into the forest and into his future.

XIV

DISCOVERY: I walked into the village in a slow hobble, concentrating on keeping my stride tight, my posture alert even though I had been badly hurt in the forest, flailing around in some forgotten dream. Past the clearing I walked into a sudden lowland which I had not noticed before, a shallow ramp laid in the mud, outlining the perimeter of the village. Past that there was a sudden rise and then the village itself, the shacks and tents unevenly laid out on the land, a long line of them flanking the corridor of a crude path which had been laid in between, the path continuing down as far as I could see and through that tunnel of vision the settlement, shacks and tents, hunts and enclosures by the hundreds, moved off into the distance and the haze.

It was the first time I had actually come into the village; all of the times before I had stood on the rim of it while waiting for Stark and Closter to bring the natives to me, while waiting for the natives to make their own shy, tentative gestures toward me. This was a commander's prerogative, to stand outside, to be approached by the natives and subordinates rather than having to approach them. I had never felt any sense of strain about this, the policies and procedures of the Bureau also being clear in this regard . . . but walking through the village I felt a vague hesitancy, the same sense of oozing disconnection which had assaulted me at other times. It was a feeling of irretrievable alienness which came over me, some aspect of the weather, the geography of the village, the silent shacks and huts in which I knew the natives were huddling, looking at me with their gaping, blank, mindless eyes . . . and not only that but the realization that my obligations, by walking in there, had been clearly defined, clearly articulated as if for the first time and that no one would save me. My fate lay within my own hands.

But hesitancy did not jar my step nor did uncertainty blind my eye. Looking casually from right to left in a swinging, cool, appraising commander's gaze, I walked down the rows of crude huts, my arms loose and dangling at my sides, my stride confident, my visage similarly so, keeping myself within the tightly controlled compass of the commander's role. My new-found self-possession caused me to move in small waves of isolation sealing me off from the natives and yet making me a part of them, a part of their village, that is to say as comprehensible and matter of fact (although very much admired) as one of their enclosures. I might have been an artifact, a feeling of being immersed in stone overcoming me as I stood poised there, letting the breezes waft their way through my appendages which felt, by the way, rather transluscent. I held my ground, my hand reaching inside my clothing to grasp and caress the weapon which lay in its accustomed place nestling cool against me. I had taken it merely for security, of course, having no intention of using it against this mild and beneficent people who had done me no harm. My actions against the mutinous and villainous crew had been for simple self-protection; if the same circumstances had been repeated I might have done it again . . . but, after all, I was not a fiend. Fiendishness, demonology, trollery lay outside of my mild compass; I was there to be reasonable. My position exuded reasonableness.

Through the open spaces of the huts I knew that natives were looking at me with emotions ranging from fear to wonder. I would, of course, be a god manifest among them; it was amusing to think that they regarded me with such awe and reverence and I allowed a small, cold godlike smile to play across my lips, at the same time spreading my legs slightly to maintain an easeful posture. My hand fell away from the comforting bulk of the weapon; knowing it was there, after all, I had no need to stroke it further. I was not a compulsive. Neither a fiend nor a compulsive. In all ways I knew that I was making exactly the impression which I had had in mind before I began this stroll, one of endless patience. I would hold my position as long as necessary. Neither moving further into the village nor going from it, I would remain there until I had achieved my objective.

It took some time. I knew that it would; I was well prepared to wait. I had, after all, nothing to do at the moment. The astonishing news from the Bureau, their refusal to allow me to debark had left me momentarily without tasks to absorb my energies. My communications with the Bureau were now at an end of course; it was not petulance but determination which had made me decide that I would never communicate with them again. If they did not understand what lay behind my very urgent and well-reasoned request to leave I was not going to discuss the issue with them any more. There would be plenty of time to settle the matter at higher levels of approval. In the meantime I bore the Bureau no grudge nor did I fulminate over their atrocious lack of sympathy or understanding. Rather I felt pity for them, a rather large and benevolent sense of pity which might well indeed have been the emotions of a disappointed but long-suffering god. They did not understand the situation; it was beneath their pitiful and limited gifts of comprehension. I bore them no ill will. It was perfectly all right with me. Everything was all right with me; I had arrived at a final and reasoned assessment of affairs which left me without any culpability whatsoever. I had done exactly what any reasonable man would have.

Some time passed. With the clicking again of invisible insects in the groves, the slow passage of the sun began across the sky, tracing out its arc in little smudged particles left behind like pencil tracings or shavings. The gentle, bucolic breezes continued to waft at my clothing, little shadows like fingers came out tentatively across the ground and tickled at my toes. I shifted my position slightly from time to time merely to keep circulation glinting and burbling through my veins, then permitted myself to stare with abstracted eyes at that inverted bowl of sky, admiring the way that it seemed to clamp down tightly upon Folsom's Planet, making an inverted bowl of all landscape. Finally and as I knew it must happen, the native called Ezekiel came down the line of shelters, moving at a slow limp, his eyes fixed upon me, moving with a steady, rolling, bouncing gait, one of his legs clearly shorter than the other (or maybe it was merely some unevennness of the ground underneath that gave this jog to his stride). He came in front of me and paused before me. He folded his hands. We stood in mutual contemplation that way for quite a while.

He did not speak nor did I; he probably out of awe, I because there was nothing for me to say until I had formulated exactly the best way to proceed. For the first time since the decision to come to the village had been made I realized that I did not know exactly how to handle the situation, did not even know what I had had in mind when I decided to come. Did I expect to ask something of Ezekiel or, rather, did I think that he would ask something of me? I was not sure. It was a matter of getting things right in my mind and in the meantime I said nothing at all. I was sure that inspiration would assert itself as it always had up until this point and that when the right series of actions had been presented, it would occur. One must have a certain faith. One must have a cold, hard faith in the efficacy of processes and even though things up until now had been difficult they had worked out for the best, hadn't they?— in a fashion of course. I knew that they would continue to do so if I only held my ground. So I stood there and so did the native; I could see up and down the line of shelters that we were being looked upon by natives observant of our actions who would not yet come out and the irony of this made me smile because in a way the natives were like the Bureau, I thought. They did not want to get involved. They did not want to take a position. They would observe, they would take in everything that had happened but they would not, of themselves, assert a position. They were not to be blamed for this of course. Considering my godlike status and the fact that only Ezekiel had been educated to communicate with me, their actions were to be expected.

Finally, Ezekiel spoke. He shuffled around in the ground, moved his feet, looked up and down at me and said, "In what way may I pay you honor?" in a very low voice. "What may I do for you?"

"I'm not a god," I said. "That's the first thing. I want you to understand that right away. None of us are gods."

"I know that now. I know that you come from a different world and that you come to help us. But the others do not know this and it is hard for me to accept this too."

"Well, you had better accept it," I said, "you had just better understand that there are no gods here and that there never have been."

"Very well," Ezekiel said after a pause. "There are no gods here."

"The others are gone," I said. "I want you to understand that as well and right now. They will not be back. They are here no longer."

He looked up at me with a bland and shy expression, his eyes showing depths of cunning that, if I were a suspicious man, might have made me feel that he did not believe me. "They have gone away?"

"They have very definitely gone away. They have left. They are no more."

"Where have they gone?" he said but slyly, lowering his eyes, "although to ask a god cannot be done . . ."

"I am not a god," I said again. "None of us are I

want to make that very clear. I want you to understand this from the beginning."

"All is well," Ezekiel said, "all is well then if you
say."

"Now you must help me," I said.

"Help you? I do not see how we can help you."

"Not *we*," I said. "Just you. I need your help."

"But I do not see how it is possible . . ."

"I told you," I said. "We are not gods . . . We are
beings such as yourselves at a more advanced state
of civilization. That is all."

"I do not know what civilization . . ."

"That need not concern you," I said. "Come with
me."

Ezekiel looked up at me, backing away slightly
from my hand, his body arched. "Go with you
where?"

"Back to the ship," I said. "I need your help."

"I do not understand."

"There is no need for you to understand. How
could you understand everything? You did not have
enough time to be told. You are to return to the ship
with me. I need your assistance."

"I am frightened," the creature said. "I am not willing to go. Something is wrong."

"Nothing is wrong at all. I need your assistance."

"I would have to consult with my people," the
creature said. "I would need the permission of the
Elders."

"That is ridiculous. You are an Elder yourself.
Furthermore *you* are a leader, otherwise you would
not be here. You are to come with me."

"But I do not want to come."

"You will come," I said again and then paused.
"You will come," I said, "because I am going to put
the equipment of knowledge in your hands. It is no
longer necessary, as the others wrongly told you, for
the others to be similarly educated, for you to go
through a period of orientation before we can turn
over to you the tools of knowledge. No, on the contrary, I have decided that you are prepared for them

now. It may be yours. If you return with me to the ship all will be given to you."

He said nothing. The cunning had returned to his face both countering and augmenting the fright in a way too peculiar, perhaps, to relate. He turned, looked back at the empty rut behind him, then back at me. "I would learn . . ."

"You will learn what you need to know. I will tell you everything. Come," I said and extended a hand, touched Ezekiel's wrist, a repellent thing to do but then I had no choice and was trying to gain his full confidence. Anything is possible if you can will yourself to do it. "You are to go with me," I said.

"Alone? With none of the others?"

"They are not necessary." My patience was beginning to wear out. I was entitled to this exhaustion of compliance; I had spent too long already trying to find cooperation through reasonable means. In terms of the terrible pressures impinging upon me I had granted more time to this than the situation deserved. Any reasonable being would have agreed with me. I reached inside my clothing once again, took out the weapon, showed it to Ezekiel. "Do you see this?" I said.

"Yes. It creates fire."

"It also creates death."

"What is death?" Ezekiel said seriously. "I do not know what you mean by that."

"It means that you will no longer be any more. It means that you will no longer exist. You will be at one with the gods. Do you understand that?"

"You mean the great pain, the pain that will not end."

"Yes, that is right."

"You are showing the great pain, the pain that will not end unless I do what you say."

"Yes," I said with relief, "that is what I am saying. I want you to go back with me."

"All right," Ezekiel said. He showed a great deal of dignity, more than would have been expected from such a loathsome creature in these circumstances. "I will go with you then, if I must."

"Yes, you must."

"May I talk to my people, first?"

"No," I said without thinking about this. "No you may not talk to them."

"They will be afraid. They will not know what has happened to me."

"That does not matter," I said. "that does not matter," and putting out a hand I seized him, took him by the glossy surfaces of his covering which felt to my hand very much like the burlap of the tents in which we had stayed and drew him toward me. He came against me quickly, softly, twisting in my gaze, then yielding spasmodically in a way that carried him almost against me and I could feel the tic of revulsion again, the evil within him contained by its alienness as it came close, then whisked past me in a spasm of foulness. I held the weapon awkwardly, jammed it then behind him. "Let us go," I said perhaps somewhat melodramatically. "Let us go now."

"I want to learn nothing."

"None of us want to learn. But you must," I said, "you have no choice, without knowledge nothing can happen," and I kicked him ahead of me then, a satisfying clout with the knee in his rectum which sent him lurching forward. Folding an arm around him I prevented him from stumbling, kicked him again and on the second kick he gave a small and terrible sound of pain which I found brutally exciting; this explosion of my will against his seemed to open me up toward new layers of feeling and that is the way we left then. Not letting him go I pushed him in front of me down the path, covering him with the weapon without letting him open up the ground. The village receded before me, spun· like tape fed through the spools into reverse. We moved down the path, skittering like animals as we came away from it and so intense was my absorption, so rigid my sense of frieze, so great my anticipation of what lay ahead that I did not even realize as I guided Ezekiel toward the forest that it had become night . . . and that throughout all of this no native had interfered by so much as his presence.

Ezekiel was right: they did think that we were gods. In my interposition, I must have fulfilled prophecy.

POLICIES AND PROCEDURES REVISITED: Upon the conclusion of the detailed and exhausting program of training, I was granted a final interview with the administrator for the project, on behalf of myself and the crew. The administrator was a small but well-chiselled man with extremely pleasant and regular features and there is absolutely no credibility to the disgusting rumours which had floated through some levels of the project that the administrators were deformed, a class of congenital cripples whose very deformities were required for them to achieve position in the program. This is the kind of malevolent and childish idiocy which one will often find in some of the partitions of the Bureau but I am happy once and for all to demolish this at the source. There was absolutely nothing wrong with the administrator in any physical sense and his mental functioning also seemed to be well within the normal range for officials of his type; all in all his credibility was very high to say nothing of his attractiveness and all statements to the contrary are just that, *statements,* words, devoid of feeling or meaning, the ethos which underlies that fashion in which we confront all of the situations of our life and how we feel as we adapt to them.

Coming into the administrator's offices I felt a shred of trepidation, not knowing exactly what was the subject of this interview, not knowing if I could deal with him in a way which would win his total respect, not even knowing what was the point or purpose of this interview, having had no experience in dealing with the administrators before. A certain feeling of increased leverage in the stomach, odd little twitches and tremors passing through my appendages quite disconcerted me but I did not know how much of this was due to nervousness and how much to the simple after effects of the training procedure which, as is well-known, is a difficult and rigorous proceeding through which only the best and toughest of the most qualified may pass. "Sit down," the administrator said, gesturing at a chair poised in an inferior position near his desk, "sit down, Folsom, we want to talk with you about the point and purpose of this voyage," and as I slid into the seat, my limbs feeling a little less watery by virtue of his attempt to so put me at ease, the administrator proceeded to tell me many of the facts and facets of the expedition to Folsom's Planet which were quite interesting and which I had never before suspected.

Some of these things I may pass on and others I may not; it was specifically pointed out that much of the material was given me in confidence and even at this stage of proceedings I would not venture to break that confidence except to say that there were aspects of the exploration of Folsom's Planet which were quite critical and surprising and made this an unusual voyage. The Bureau, it seemed, was not totally confident about its position and had been under pressure recently. Increasing objections to the program of the Federation from many quarters had put the Bureau on the defensive for the first time in many many years.

Some of the opposition of course were referring to the program not as one of amalgamation but of "conquest," the brutalization of innocent worlds to bring them into the hands of the Federation, render their natives hostage, their resources as plunder. Although everyone connected with the Bureau knew that this was untrue—why, the Federation had no plans for "conquest" at all, all that the Federation was trying to do was to make the universe a safe and agreeable place in which all of the races could live equably and without fear of one another—the opposition had managed to sow the seeds of discontent at many levels of the populace and there was talk even now of somehow "limiting" the Federation, of "undercutting" the Bureau, of even, incredibly, dismantling the policies and procedures of contact which had been so successful for hundreds of years and had made the universe such a kind and accessible extension of our everyday reality.

Yes, the Bureau knew that what the opposition had to say was tripe, that the opposition had set upon this line of argument only so that it could utilize discontent to put itself in the position of the Bureau. Rather than dismantling, it was quite clear that these people wanted to *seize* the instruments of the Federation for themselves, turn them to their own ends and it was only the determination of the Bureau, its courage and its integrity so to speak which functioned as interposition between the advanced, benign, smooth-running civilization which we had at present and the ten thousand centuries of paganism and barbarism to which the opposition would cheerfully revert us if only given the chance.

The administrator's little hands twitched as he said this and his tiny eyes bulged, his well-chiselled and well-formed features betrayed a kind of agitation which would not have been suspected at repose although the shimmer of emotions across his face was so fluid that only one as alert to them as myself would have even noticed. "And now we come to the crucial part of this," the administrator said in his high but pleasantly well-modulated voice, "the point which is the most serious and which I had to prepare you for by giving you this little bit of background."

"I'm listening," I said, "I'm very interested in this. Of course I don't think that there's any concern, the opposition is quite weak and isolated and you can be sure that *I* have never accepted . . ."

"More cunning than you would think," the administrator murmured, "and far more determined as well but that is not the point. The point is this: it is very possible that the opposition, clever and cunning in all of its operations although very weak by numbers, may have actually infiltrated into the Bureau itself, into the *very crew* . . ."

"Do you mean that one of *us* might be a traitor?" I asked, rather astounded. "That sounds highly unlikely, considering the rigor of the training processes . . ."

"It *is,*" the administrator said quickly. "It is highly unlikely that they would have actually infiltrated anyone into the crew and of course the screening processes are quite rigorous. So is the training for that matter; it is extremely doubtful that anyone of the opposition who are a congenitally inferior group could pass through the difficult system which we have evolved for training." He cast a quick, darting glance from one side of the room to the other, his eyes rolling. "However," he said, "you must take all precautions. You cannot be too protective of your position in these difficult times and you must be aware of all the possibilities. We have to take precautions; we have to be aware that the enemy is all around us. He is cunning, he is fierce, he is barbaric as the barbarians themselves and he will give us no quarter. Accordingly," the administrator said, "we must face the possibility that they might have managed to work one of their number into the crew and have survived the training process. Do you understand?"

"Of course I understand," I said, lowering my voice instinctively as the administrator made gestures with his wrists reminding me that the very conversations one might have in the Bureau, even under the tightest security, might be monitored. "I'm aware of that. Still . . . what would their objective be?"

"What would their objective be? What do you think that they would do?—why the treacherous scum," the administrator said, his hands shaking their way up and down the desk as if he were playing an instrument, "would do everything within their power to sabotage the mission. They would stop at nothing."

"Yes," I said, "I agree with that. Nevertheless, what

must I be alert for? What route would their treachery take? What would they do?"

"I'll tell you what they'd do," the administrator said, his voice breaking. He leaned forward, putting a hand at the side of his mouth behind which he whispered, "they'd arrange to place our technological materials in the hands of the barbarians without first socializing them, that's what they'd do. That's what the filthy scum believe, that the socialization process is repressive, that it's merely a means of turning the barbarians into a slave class after which we can move in with our technological superiority and take over their planet, use them as cheap labor. Isn't that disgusting?"

"Of course it is."

"That's the kind of swill they're disseminating," the administrator said, pounding the desk with a splayed palm, wincing as it drove spikes of contact up his arm, "and that's what we've got to consider when we're dealing against them. They do not understand that the socialization process is intrinsic to the gift of technology, that we cannot turn it over to barbarians until they have been helped to reach a better and more moral understanding of life."

"Of course," I said. This was a return to known ground; we had been through it in the training sessions and very much to the point they had been indeed. Who could think that we were oppressing the aliens when we were actually functioning selflessly to elevate them?

"So you will have to watch them very carefully," the administrator said. "The crew that is to say. You should be aware at all times that it is possible that one of the opposition has infiltrated. You must be aware to all danger, alert to the full range of possibility. You have been selected for commander precisely because of all known candidates you showed the highest potential for alertness, for being aware of the thieves and spies, liars and poltroons in our midst." The administrator's hands had taken on a fine tremble, little fine droplets of spray seemed to be coming off them in the quivering, causing a halo to encircle those palms and as he pushed himself away from the desk, a corner of his chair must have dug uncomfortably in the floor causing him to stop in mid-wrench with an astonished expression; then, his body overbalancing, he saved himself from toppling to the floor only by frantically placing a palm on the arm of the chair, heaving himself to an upright position. "Do you see what I mean?" he said. "They're all over. Their agencies are surrounding us at all times. You cannot be too careful with them, you must take precautions." He stood uncomfortably, weaving slightly, took a handkerchief from his pocket and very carefully wiped the top of the desk, then the arms of the chair. "They also infiltrate their bacteria," he said, "they have a very highly subtle and sophisticated bacteriological attacking system which they have developed to the point where they can put poisonous microbeings throughout even our most private chambers. But," he said, folding the handkerchief and putting it into his pocket decisively, "but, we have methods of our own. As long as we maintain alertness, as long as we know of their foul, vicious and heinous means we cannot be defeated."

"Yes," I said. I admit that I was somewhat shaken. The true dimensions of the opposition's threat, the foul lengths to which they would go to impose their evil view of existence upon the mild and undicatatorial Bureau confused me and caused me to feel at the pit of my firm and well-muscled commander's stomach a sting of apprehension which, like an insect, seemed to flutter about, giving small bites. "Is there anything else?" I said. I did not, by saying this, indicate any impatience with what the administrator had to say or any disinclination to continue hearing from him the true nature of the enemy. All that I wanted to indicate to him—and this I am certain is the truth —was that if he had nothing more to say to me on this or other topics I would find it far better to go away from there, to meditate upon these dangerous images by myself, the true and dreadful possibilities which the opposition would send with us to accompany the flight and sleepers to the void. This touched off another chain of speculation and I turned to the administrator who was already standing. I watched him pat his handkerchief into place in his pocket; his face was set in a firm and disciplined line, giving no indication—as well he should not—of the facts of treachery which had been unreeled before me. I asked him, "What are we going to do during the period of unconsciousness? Will that not be very dangerous, to allow them the ship while none of us are in a position to deal with them?"

"That is a very good point," the administrator said somewhat shakily. "We have considered that and we have, accordingly, put into action, a new policy. One of you will remain awake at all times. The period of unconsciousness will be in shifts; you will alternate. One of you will be awake at all times. In that way there will always be an alert presence upon the ship."

"I see," I said. "If there are four of us then each of us will remain awake for a six month period . . ."

"Something like that," the administrator said, "perhaps not exactly that long since you must all be conscious and functioning for a period after takeoff and for a time before debarkation. Perhaps it will be four or five months. That is being worked out by the statisticians."

"But that's not quite fair," I said, "because it means that during that time the biological clock will keep on working, it means that we will, each of us, lose a certain period of precious time . . ." and then I trailed off embarrassed, seeing the great glare from the administrator's eyes, looking at the fluorescence which came off the spare furnishings of the stark rooms in a particularly threatening fashion as if not only he but the machinery of the Bureau itself were responding to my unthinking and rather treacherous response. "Of course it's a small sacrifice to protect us against the evil possibilities of the opposition," I said quickly.

The administrator nodded once, stiffly. "We thought

114

you would think so," he agreed, "and now I believe that our interview is at a close. Unless you have anything else to say, of course."

"I have nothing else to say," I said with a rigid formality, invoking my commander's discipline. I stood, moved toward the doorway, stood there uncomfortably looking at the administrator who, convulsively, assumed once again his position behind the desk. He seemed to be in a continued state of agitation, bending, opening and closing hidden drawers rapidly, the clatter like a dry series of coughs, but I felt no need to add to his disturbance at this time. "Very well," I said, "excuse me," and went through the door then, pulling it closed firmly behind not only to shut myself quickly from sight of the administrator but—this must be admitted—to shut him off from me. I did not want to look at him any more, at least until the last preflight breathing. His presence had suddenly become disturbing for reasons I could not quite phrase.

Slowly, meditatively, I walked down the halls then and back to the special section in which the crew was quartered awaiting their own final instructions before debarkation. They all asked me, of course, what the administrator had wanted to talk to me about.

I did not answer them. I explained nothing. I let no information drop.

I knew that the administrator would have wanted it that way.

XVI

RECAPITULATION AND EPIPHANY: Folsom, with his highly developed and acute sense of the developing realities of the situation had known from the beginning that Stark was the villain, the corruptor from the opposition smuggled through the training processes into the crew. Stark or Closter but probably Stark because Folsom just had an instinct that it would have to be him. From Stark the poison and corruption had then spread, infecting the others so that soon the entire crew was arrayed against him and only Folsom himself remained as the bulwark of sanity and righteousness. It was a pity that the Bureau could not have understood this, could not have leaped to an appreciation of the situation to equal Folsom's own but the explanation for that was obvious as well. The opposition had managed to infiltrate the Bureau and were destroying their policies and procedures. Folsom's desperate messages, instead of reaching the proper authorities were being intercepted at the point of communications intercept and destroyed, then false messages were being turned back. But the original villainy was obviously perpetrated by Stark. He had been responsible for everything. From him the poisons had leaked out. That was the way it had been. Nothing else to say. The poisons would have infected the powerful and dependable Folsom himself if he had not been, by virtue of his great strength and commander's position, above being so easily manipulated. Actually, it was surprising that he had survived this, managed to dispose of the villains. The Bureau would surely be

116

proud of him . . . if only he could get his position over to them.

Stumbling briskly through the forest again with Ezekiel, the alien pattering along behind him like a faithful if friendless dog, big tears of rain falling absently around him, colliding with the mud like petals, Folsom felt the need to once again discuss this with the alien, make his position clear. It was unfortunate that he did have to talk about it with Ezekiel, almost anyone else would have been better but his choices were severely limited and the alien, at least, could understand. The murderous crew had given him enough equipment to do that.

"It was all Stark, that's what I figure," Folsom said, not turning but making his voice very loud and distinct so that not a word would be missed, not with the sizzling sound of the rain, "it all started with him. Closter and that woman, that bitch Nina, they came right along with it, they were weakminded and treacherous from the start but the one who began it was Stark. How did he slip through? I asked them that but they wouldn't answer. They won't say anything to me now."

"Nothing," Ezekiel said after a while. "Nothing." His footsteps kept measured pace with Folsom's. Folsom was no fool, he was listening for those footsteps every step of the way: if he had heard them cease or even break their rhythm for an instant he would have taken out his weapon and shot the native as he had shot all of the other treacherous slugs. But those footsteps slammed away behind him like Folsom's own conscience, as regular as his breath; he knew that he would have no difficulty with the creature. "Nothing at all."

"You know why they won't say anything to me now?" bellowed Folsom and without waiting for the creature to reply said, "because they know how dangerous I am, because they know that I'm onto the truth. The whole world, almost all of it, is controlled by the opposition and they're going to take their deceit to the stars, seed the stars with their deceit, that's it . . . but they know that I know their plan and they can't stop me. That's why they won't answer. What do you think of that?"

The alien said nothing and Folsom felt constrained to halt, turn on the thing and show his weapon. "What do you think of that?" he said again. He did not mean to threaten; he was only trying to have a reasonable conversation.

"I think not. I do not know. I do not know about the affairs of the gods."

"And that's another thing," Folsom said, "I want you to stop that right now. We aren't gods. We're ordinary fellows just like all of you are, just at a more advanced technological level. We're here to help you."

"I don't know what you're talking about," Ezekiel said. He leered at Folsom with his characteristic look of stupidity, the alien did, but Folsom could tell from the use of the familiar contraction that the alien was not nearly so dull as he wished to appear, that he might indeed have been proselytized by the faithless barbarians who trained it into the same treacherous point of view. Folsom knew that this was a possibility, being no fool at all, but had no choice, granted all the circumstances, but to continue to deal with the creature. After he had finished with him, after he had done what was necessary, a different approach might be possible and Folsom had plans, he had a great number of plans, but for the moment he had to face the alien, put up with his own deceit. Ezekiel made a motion which Folsom found uninterpretable, an absent wave of his hand as if he were signalling someone and then he began to move once again. Folsom put out a hand to halt the alien and then, thinking the better of it, turned and preceded him. There was no point in getting into a dispute. It had all gone beyond that.

"None of this is my fault, you know," Folsom said, "I'm not responsible. I was just trying to do a job. The others wouldn't let me. None of them understood that it had to be done my way. None of them ever accepted that."

He was babbling, Folsom thought. He was beginning to lose his control of language. Perhaps it would be better to keep quiet. Perhaps he should let the responsibility for explanation shift from him to elsewhere; he could not do it all himself. It was not expected. Folsom found himself thinking, for the first time, of a higher power: not the Bureau, some power even higher than that controlling and shaping his actions on which he could rely in this moment of great difficulty. He could not do all of this himself. It was not right that all of it should devolve upon him. There should be someone or something else which would take over the responsibility and in the name of everything, silently, Folsom evoked it. Really, he had been driven quite to the limits of his ability to function. Too many pressures had descended upon him and even though he had managed to fight off all of them one by one, solving each problem as it was thrust upon him, he was now approaching his limits. How much more of this can he take? Folsom thought, crashing foot by foot through the forest. Was it fair for him to be put through all of this? He had always despised self-pity but at this moment he discovered that it was the glue which can piece a failing personality together. Now, he really did not know what he would do without it.

He kept on through the forest; it was only half a mile or so now to their ship. They had set down two miles from the village; Folsom had wanted to be closer but this had been Stark's idea when they had circled the planet in low, close order, hovering then above this village for several cycles while the decision' was being made. Stark had felt that putting down closer to the village than the two mile gap would be dangerous; frightening to the natives, dangerous to the village itself because of the heat of the engines, the fragmentation of impact and though Folsom had known that this was nonsense: the new equipment according to the Bureau was both cool

119

and self-contained. Still he had not been anxious to overrule Stark with whom he had been trying to get along (at that time). He had been trying to get along with all of them in fact; the result was that they had put down two miles from the village, even more than two miles, and every time they had wanted contact with the natives they had to undertake that stumbling walk through the forest and after the contacts with the natives there was the stumbling walk *back,* back and forth through the forest, lumbering through the density and the mud, why it was enough to depress anyone; it would have taken the edge off anyone's spirit to put up with that kind of hike just to make a routine contact. No wonder they had been unable to establish a real relationship with the village, no wonder things had been so difficult: the physical act of separation had meant that they would arrive at the village in a state of nausea. It all came clear to Folsom then. It was coming clearer all the time; it was a *plot,* that was what it was; a plot which Stark and Closter had worked out from the start in order to make contact as difficult as possible, in order to isolate *Folsom* from their plans . . . well, he had taken care of that, Stark and Closter were no longer his concern but if he had only known then what he deduced now it would not have gotten this far.

"There's going to be an end to this," he said to Ezekiel, "there's going to be an end to it right now, all of this is coming to a climax, I tell you, I don't have to put up with this any more," and maybe the alien said something or maybe he did not; it did not matter to Folsom, the alien was absolutely intrinsic to his plans now, to his new-found insight.

The ship loomed up before them; he could see it through a break in the trees and seeing it that way, arched up into that engraved porcelain bowl of sky, Folsom could understand as if for the first time why the aliens might indeed think of them as gods, as the Thunder Gods, indeed the aspect of that ship looming, the way it must have appeared to them screaming fire as it circled in low orbit, spreading

120

heat and fumes within its parameter of flame . . . why it must have been an enormous experience for these aliens, simple folk all, primitives, living on the lowest level of expectation and insight . . . and yet here was this ship, this great chariot of the sky rolling in before them . . . yes, Folsom could understand this. For the first time he felt a respect for the aliens, for tormented Ezekiel himself, it must have been a very difficult thing to go through. Considering everything they had shown unusual courage. And then Folsom found himself beginning to laugh in uneven, expectorative fashion, his frame shaking with the explosion of little coughs, flutters near his chest . . . who was he to sentimentalize the aliens when the aliens had hardly sentimentalized him? Well, that was a thought. All of this was interesting. All of it demanded further consideration; a shame that he would not have the time to pursue this line of thought through to its logical end. No time for that. Leave it be. Let it go.

The rain was falling more heavily now, the drops inflating to the size, Folsom thought, of saucers, the space between them also widening however so that Folsom had the sensation of a man walking *between* the drops literally cleaving out a space through the elements in which he could pass untouched; a strange feeling of power in this apprehension. Walk through water. And the waters will pass aside. He passed the enclosure in which Stark and Closter had been without a trace of emotion, keeping his face tightly controlled with his captain's facade. He had already passed the place where he had last seen Nina without response whatsoever. Gone. Purged out. He was beyond feeling.

In the shadow of the ship, the drops spattering around him, exploding on the ground like pieces of china, Folsom stopped. He turned toward Ezekiel. The alien came up behind him in a fast scuttle, then stopped at Folsom's gesture, hanging on the terrain in a frozen posture. Folsom looked at him and he

121

nodded. He felt in the alien's submission the power beginning. Conditions were right.

He pointed toward the ship. "Go inside," he said, "get in there."

"But I must . . ."

"Get in there," Folsom said loudly, his finger not wavering. Ezekiel shrugged. Then slowly, delicately, high on his toes, his gnarled little body bobbing, he passed Folsom and hit the first step of the ramp leading into the ship. Step by step he ascended. Folsom watched him. The alien passed through the first open lock and into the safety zone.

Only then did Folsom follow him, his attention concentrated into that little black well through which the alien had passed.

In the small cell of decontamination he would meet him. They would pass through the gates and into the ship together. And then, in the abcess of the ship . . .

. . . Well, then, there would be an end to it.

XVII

NINA'S WHISPER: Now another part of it comes back: lying against her in that shelf of forest, huddled against her, making of my body a canvas for her against the cold, I held her very quietly for a long time in the aftermath of intercourse, resting first one cheek and then the other tentatively against her, feeling the smooth and even panels of her back, and unassaulted by all of my hammering, her body is as impermeable as a wound pressed against me. Rolling then, finally, to look up at the sky, my body relaxing, falling like a balloon to the ground, bouncing once, then lying still beside her.

She said, "Something is terribly wrong here." Always in the aftermath of fucking she wanted to talk. That might have been the real reason for all of the trouble. If only she had kept silent . . . but she would not. She would not keep silent and I did not even know until later how badly I wanted this to be.

"What?" I said, "what is wrong here?"

"We shouldn't be. It shouldn't be."

"Don't," I said, "don't start that again, please," and ran a finger up and down her forearm, hoping to distract her, willing my resilient commander's frame into strong dismissal. "I can't bear to talk about it."

"Something is wrong. What are we doing here? We're not here to help them."

I should have left. I should have stepped up and away from her, moved into the forest, gone back to my private commander's enclosure and thought about this or nothing for hours until the sun filled the forest and we were beyond the mood of the night. But I

123

did not do so. I did not do this. I was a fool. I stayed with her.

"Of course we're here to help them. We're here to civilize them and bring them into the Federation."

"But what is the Federation?"

"The Federation is everywhere," I said, "the Federation controls all of the races of man and tries to bring those that are not into this mutual compact."

"Those are lies," she said. Her skin was very warm. "We know nothing of that at all."

"Of course we do."

"No," she said, "no we do not. We have never seen the Federation. All that we know of it is what the Bureau tells us that it is."

"The Bureau and the Federation are the same. The Bureau is the agent of the Federation on this earth and through the Bureau the Federation works its will . . ."

"No," she said again, "no, we do not know that. We only know of the Bureau and what the Bureau does. They tell us that there is a Federation but we have no evidence. All that we have is what they say."

Treasonous. This was treasonous talk and I should have left her. The warning of the administrator slid face up into my brain as if inscribed on a cool stone slab: I read the words of that warning as they pressed against the surfaces of the dura mater, graven and terrible. "Please," I said, "stop talking this way." I wanted to leave her but I could not. Something held me to her that way on the floor of the forest. I cupped her skin under my palm, felt it bunched and gathered there. Against my will I felt the old slick rising below. "Please stop it," I said again and almost began to speak to her of the administrator and his warning but something held me back, something strong and disciplined, beating within my great commander's heart. I was no fool; I would not tell her everything.

"You only want me to stop because you can't bear to think this way," she said. "That's what they do to us; they prevent us from thinking, they make the very act of thought, anything they won't allow us, evil and monstrous. But it's not so. We have a right. I have a right to say this. How do we know that the Federation exists?"

'If there were no Federation there would be no Bureau. We know that."

"Do we? Do we really know this to be the truth? What do we know except what they tell us. We have no right to be sure until it is the truth."

"Have you been talking to the others?" I said. I could not help myself; I began to roll in her direction, rested belly to belly. "Have you?"

"All of us have been talking about this."

"All of you? When?"

"All of the time," she said. "All the time," she said again vaguely and then said nothing at all; her hands, prowlers, began to work up and down my sides, pulling me close against her. "Don't talk any more," she said raggedly. "Just . . ."

But I was not to be put off. "You started this," I said, "I didn't want to talk, you did. Now it's too late." I rolled from her. In the dull thump with which I hit the earth she might have sensed my fury. Perhaps not. "What have you been talking about?"

"I told you," she said after a pause, "I told you all that already."

"You should not . . ."

"Why?" she said loudly, "why shouldn't we?" and then as if the bonds of control had snapped said, "We're not permitted to talk, we're not permitted to have certain thoughts, they won't let us say or think what we want to . . . *why?* What are they afraid of? I don't think that the Bureau has our best interests at heart, they're not trying to help us or anyone, they're just shutting off . . ."

"They are not," I said, thinking of the administrator's warning. "They are not . . ."

"Oh go away. I can't talk to you either. You just don't want to hear the truth."

"And what is this truth? What is this truth you keep on talking about?"

125

"Isn't it obvious?" she said, "don't you see what it is?"

"No. I don't."

"They're out to control," she said, "they're out to make slaves of the universe."

I was astounded. The flat madness of it quite unlocked my senses; they seemed to spin. Totally subjective disorientation of course; I had been through it on the training exercises. I was capable, then, of dealing with it. "You're insane," I said. "That's not anything you should say."

"It's the truth."

"It is not the truth. It is insane. The Federation and its instrument, the Bureau, exist only to preserve the peaceable, equable distribution of intelligent civilized races within . . ."

"No," she said. Abruptly she stood, coming to her feet like a revealed secret in the gloom, the white panels of her body bobbing in front of me and I felt the vague stirrings of thwarted lust which I knew then only as regret. "No, you won't listen. They were quite right. I said that you could be talked to . . ."

"Who was right?"

She shook her head. "You haven't heard a thing, have you?" she said, "not a thing that has been said to you, all that you listen to is yourself. You fool."

"Who was right?" I said again. "The others?"

"I won't talk to you any more," she said. She stooped for her garments, gathered them to her. "There's nothing to say. It's hopeless."

I lay on the ground. Perhaps I should have stood to pursue her but I could not will myself into effort. It simply did not seem to be worth it. This was my mistake. "You've all been conspiring against me," I said quietly. My control was admirable. Had I been a dispassionate observer I would have been stricken with admiration for it. "Right from the beginning."

"Hopeless," she said again, "you're unable to understand anything."

"I understand a good deal. I understand more than

you do. I'm charged with doing that; I'm the commander, remember? What does the rock say?"

"What?" she said. She had almost moved out of range, but she came now from behind the grey trunk of one of the fat, enormous trees which filled Folsom's Forest on Folsom's Planet. "What did you say?"

"I asked you what was written on the rock. Remember? You were going to work on it."

"I didn't work on it," she said. "We've got far more important things to do than to worry about strange writing on a rock. Where did you find it anyway?"

"You know where I found it," I said. "I told you. You mean, you haven't even looked at it?"

"No," she said, "I have not. Maybe some other time."

"When?"

"I don't know."

"Come here," I said. "I want you to come here." I do not quite know what was on my mind but I arched upwards, sat uncomfortably, my hands on my knees. "I said come here."

She shook her head slowly. "No," she said, "I'm never going to come there again. It's all finished, don't you understand that?"

"Understand what?"

"You're a fool," she said, "first the rock and then the conspiracy and then this. Don't you ever listen to anyone? Don't you know what your Bureau is trying to do to all of us? Don't you understand that?"

"No," I said, "I do not. I don't know what you're talking about," and I did not, this much was the truth, I had no idea whatever what she was trying to say and it was puzzlement which yanked me to my feet, confusion which set one foot before the other, sheer astonishment which set one foot after the other in a lurching stride that carried me toward her. I did not know what I wanted to do but the impulse was clear; I wanted to draw her against me and do something grand yet ferocious, something blended out of need and rage, some complex action that would simultaneously wrench her around and force her to

127

confront me for the first time, force her to see what I was, the responsibility I bore, the dignity to which I was entitled . . . and the fact of my nakedness did not undercut this dignity but, I thought, added credibility to it: seeing me in this primal and natural state would she not be further moved, would she not regret what she had said to me, her total failure of understanding? But it was not only the desire for pity which sent me stumbling after her but something quite stronger to which I did not want to give a name; I suppose that I wanted to hurt her badly —looking back upon all of this now I am capable of admitting my weakness, the weakness that moved within me no less than any of the others, the desire to *hurt*—and she must have seen this, must have seen all of it in strange, glinting shudders and flashes of the accursed moonlight; with one quiet, controlled shriek she turned and vanished into the forest, infinitely more graceful than I and inflamed by an urgency no less great she was soon out of touch, out of reach . . . and no fool I, at the first battering contact of branch against cheek, the first premonitory stumble on sudden stone which yanked me into the mud, I stopped. I knew that she was gone; I knew that it was beyond me. I would never be able to touch her again.

But if I would not be able to touch her there would, at least, be something else, I thought, something that could be done instead to reach her and the thought of this helped me to turn slow and cunning in the wood, I came into a crouch then, wiping fingers across my face, looking to anyone who might have been observing this (but no one observed it, no one, ever) like a statue or figurine, a mask of contemplation there and then. In that cramped position, with the first slivers of pain beginning to come into me I had a vision, a genuine vision, the first and only one of my life (to that point; now I have visions all of the time, everything has changed but there must be a first for everything) and it was overwhelming: it hit me in the plexus like a fist in dazzle of light, accretion of sound, intake of breath. Spread out before me then I saw all of Folsom's Planet as it would be when the socialization process was complete. After Stark and Closter had done their careful and plodding work, had sown the seed of technology amidst the natives, had worked them toward their position in the great Federation, Folsom's Planet appeared to me as it would then be and it was as if I knew every crevice of it, so familiar was its aspect. Looking at the cities, the rampways, the grave centers and the slaughtering houses, I saw not only the Planet but the world itself and that world was one I had already possessed, it was in fact, identical to my own life and there was no way, absolutely no way, in which this could be changed.

This reconstructed Folsom's Planet, this Folsom's Planet of both history and future, burst upon me in colors, odor, sound and touch and it would be convenient to say and would fit well into place to say that this vision drove me absolutely mad and I have not been the same since except that this is not so: it would be an absolute lie, my commander's intelligence, my captain's integrity and strength of will are absolute and nothing, nothing, nothing could shake them. Never, never, never, never, never. Kill, kill, kill, kill, kill, kill.

XVIII

TOPPING OUT: In the bowels of the ship I heard Ezekiel's breath before me, coming as if from a great distance although he was only a few feet behind me; then as I hit the switches to seal the locks, bring the lighting to full power, proportions became realigned in the familiar way and he stood before me, separated only by two or three yards, standing there awkwardly as the ship blazed around him. His simple, barbarian's eyes widened with wonder as he took in the aspect of the ship, its cool, technological wonders, the sterile beauty of its steel bulkheads. Fear was overcome by this involvement. I could see working within him the conflict between terror and the desire to touch and finally he raised a hand in a tentative way, brushing it against the steel, then dropped it to his side and stared at me. "It is beautiful," he said.

"Yes. It is."

"It is very beautiful. It is the temple of the gods."

"No," I said, "you are wrong. We are not gods. This is not a temple."

He lowered his eyes to the gleaming surfaces underneath. "To me you are gods," he said, "this is what I see. I see the thunder chariots and from them walk the gods with great power and strength. They come into our world and as the prophecies have held they come bearing gifts."

"No," I said, "we are not gods. There is no prophecy. There is no world." I took off my outer clothing, allowing it to fall around me to the gleaming disin-

130

fected surfaces. Ezekiel remained in place. "Come," I said, "come with me."

"I am frightened."

"There is nothing to frighten you."

"But I am," he said, "I am," and he remained in place. I could see the thin shaking beginning around the upper surfaces of his body, then moving upward and down, his eyes rolling in his head, almost imperceptible but quite obvious to one as skilled in reactive psychology as I. After a while, however, the shaking modulated and he remained then unmoving as I stood patiently giving him no reason for increased fear. I waited for him to speak.

"I am less frightened," he said.

"Good," I said, keeping my voice gentle, "I am glad of that."

Then I turned, extended a hand, gestured to show him that I wanted him to follow and then, moving down the slick pathways of the ramp, I moved toward its very center.

Downward we plunged, through layers of wires and tubing, past coils and condensers and into the secret, throbbing machinery of the ship itself, the low hum of the maintenance circuit giving it only a minimal lighting as we moved into the center. The ship was alive yet dead; to bring its engines and fluorescence to full power would have taken hours of the most sophisticated efforts aided, of course, by the opening of circuits from the Bureau . . . but Bureau had been stubborn, they would not allow us to debark so all of our efforts would have gone in vain. The ship was neither alive nor dead but in a ground in between where it could not function. At the bottom I looked up at the alien, unsteadily making his way by grasping the railings, and felt a surge of sympathy for him: if the ship was terrifying to me then how must it look to him, a simple primitive from a barbaric civilization? Terrifying, that was how it must be. In a sudden twitch of consciousness I could see it as he must, then: a strange tube hung with machinery, machinery dripping in coils

131

and wires from the enclosure, the dank smell of machinery swirling up from the inmost and secret heart of the ship, and leading him into this darkness was the Thunder God of the chariot . . . oh, I could see it clearly, this sudden shift of consciousness, the placing of my consciousness into his so that we were for the moment identical, the two of us merged into a shell which became one being . . . one very discontented being of course.

But downward into the ship now, my purpose overwhelming the dislocation and so then I lost sight of Ezekiel's consciousness being concerned fundamentally and as always with my own. We came through a series of ramps and stairs into the huge, bleak room at the pit of the ship lighted by only the thin glow of fluorescence, with the dark hum of the transistors the only sound in all of these spaces and it was there at last where I halted him, motioning him with a gesture to move back against one of the walls while I stood across from him.

He looked up cautiously, his simple, primitive's face falling open into wonder as he saw the sheer, clear rising of the ship, the vaulting of spaces up hundreds of feet, the sheer dimensions of it overwhelming him as very much it should have and I felt once again the commander's pride: I had been in control of all of this.

This mighty ship had been at my pleasure; I had slept in it, guided it, taken the responsibility for the landing. Whatever else had happened they could not take this away from me. Neither Stark nor Closter, not even Nina had guided the ship. I had.

"Do you see this?" I said to Ezekiel unnecessarily. Of course he saw it. Still, I felt that I had to establish a certain mood. "Do you?"

"Yes," he said quietly, "I see it. I . . ."

"This is the ship in which we came. It is not a chariot."

He said nothing. If his face had had any intelligence it would have held cunning. Slowly, almost imperceptibly, he nodded.

"And this," I said and paused, then went on with it because not to have done so would have been a negation of whatever had brought us here, "this is the place at the bottom of the ship where all the knowledge is held. Do you understand that?"

He nodded slowly, spread his palms in a gesture strangely reminiscent of that of one of the crew (I cannot remember which, they already are beginning to jumble in my mind) and held his position. "The place of knowledge?" he said.

"Here," I said, "here are kept the secrets that would have been given your people when you were prepared to receive them. Here are the secrets which would give you great machines, the secrets of fire, the means by which you could control . . ."

"What are machines?" Ezekiel said, "I do not understand this."

"But you would have," I said, "you would have understood all of that, if the plans had gone ahead." I paused, looked at him. "You may still have it now," I said. "Do you want to know?"

"I want to go home. I want to go back to my people."

"Yes," I said, "yes, that is true, you want to go back to your people and so do I, back to mine, but this cannot be done. We have the same problem; we are both separated from our people, you and I, but that does not have to counsel absolute despair; if we are separated, we can return, if we have been torn asunder, we can heal unto the breach and in the long run, good faith will run out. Here," I said, shambling over to one of the lockers, pressing a recessed switch in the wall causing it to fall open, a switch which no one but I would have known about, knowledge of that switch being restricted to the commander himself, that is to say the man who bears the full responsibility for the well-being of the crew on the voyage as well as the security of its documents, "here," I said again and took out of the locker an armful of documents, brandished them, then walked over and put them on the pit of his stomach forcing Ezekiel with a puzzled, terrified expression to bring his arms down, gather them in. "This is what you want," I said, "and this is therefore what you will have. Eventually you would have gotten them anyway, but this is quicker, don't you think? Besides it's more convenient that way." I reached into the locker, brushed aside more documents, my hands fluttering away in the darkness until they had set upon what I had wanted and then I took it; this I gave to Ezekiel, a duplicate of the very weapon bouncing and jouncing within my own clothing. "This too," I said, dropping it into one of the crude pouches sewn on his clothing while he backed away from me, "this is what you really wanted, isn't it? Well, you may have that too. A destruction machine, a killing machine and the only thing we ask in return is that you read up on the documents. It's all there. Everything is there."

"I don't understand," he said once again. Failure of understanding seemed to be our only common ground . . . but that in itself can be sufficient, of course. "I don't know what you're doing."

"In those papers are everything you need to know," I said, motioning to the documents which slipped and poured from his hands like little animals as he staggered to hold onto them, and had to bend to pick up stray wisps, "Machinery. Fire. *Controlled* fire. Munitions. The wheel. Gunpowder. Steam. Light. The internal combustion engine if you're sophisticated enough to follow through the diagrams. Geometry, Euclidean and non-Euclidean. The three laws of thermodynamics. Nuclear fission. Controlled mutation. *Uncontrolled* mutation. It's all there, you're holding it!"

He shook his head. "I am frightened. I don't want it."

"Well," I said, "well yes, maybe you don't want it, that's a very good point and I appreciate your having made it but you see, whether you want it or not makes very little difference to us. We travelled light years to put it into your hands, all under our benevolent control of course, and I'm afraid that your wishes and opinions have very little to do with the situation at this time. You're going to have to take it just as we did, you see."

"I don't . . ."

"But," I said with awful patience, "but look here now," crouching so that I could confront the thing at his own height, *"we* didn't want it either, did we? We would have been just as well without it, all of us, we just inherited it. We didn't have any choice in the matter; they gave it to us and we just had to do what we could with it but don't you think given a choice we would have passed it up?"

He backed away from me. Documents jiggled in his arms but he held them in tight embrace, a powerful, equivocal point of balance. I knew that he would not drop them. He could not let them go. "Come," I said, "let me take you out of here. Go back to your people. Take them back to your shamans; teach them the language and they'll find some very interesting material here. You won't regret it."

"I won't regret it. I do not understand . . ."

"Of course," I said, "of course you don't understand. What the hell does that have to do with it? The entire human condition comes from a failure of understanding, do you think that you're the first to have that?" and so on and so forth. "It makes no difference, makes no difference," I shouted as I ascended the ramp, the two of us coming out of the bowels of the ship, moving toward that snout now as if we were rising through levels of prehistoric mire (I have a rather metaphoric turn of mind sometimes) toward some recapitulation of all history, spinning through the grave of the ship then and up its spout toward the high rising cone, the two of us scuttling on the ramps and I did not know then who preceded who in that climb: sometimes he was ahead of me, I thought, and at other times he might have been behind; entering into his consciousness again with that shift of perception, I knew that he could see it the same way. Was I follower or leader? Was I apparition leading him out or doppelganger pursuing him, probing and limiting his flight? Ezekiel did not know, I did not know either, and so through steel and glass, the alien grunting and scrambling behind, we continued.

We continued through the ship for a thousand years; through ice and fire we ascended. Gleaming little daggers of light, cast from broken places in the fuselage where the weapon had struck through, were lighting our way and it was in that millenium as if we were not two but one, one great, shambling beast split into halves, groaning, screaming, grunting for the light as we trembled upward. He was I, I he and through ten centuries we exchanged not only shouts and footsteps, we exchanged the very ethos itself in the vault of the great beast scrambling and through it all with some calm, cold, piercing part of the brain that cast the great strobe of light forward, I told myself to have patience, patience, you will emerge from this, this is only as long as you want to make it and knowing this . . . knowing that I could at any time call it to an end, make both Ezekiel and ship disappear, was what enabled me to bear it for ten centuries. To have within my hands the means of reversal was, then, to bear what was inflicted upon us and I did not faint nor did I crumple under these burdens but instead only continued, upward on the ramp, holding hard on the poles that gripped our hands like ropes until finally we came into the place of the vault where we had entered and only then did the halves of us split, fission then like mitosis, the beast splitting to parts that were named Ezekiel and Folsom and there we stood, separate once again, looking at one another. In his hands he gripped what I had given him.

"Go," I said.

He looked at me. There was no need for him to say anything; we had been one person, now two only in the flesh; the need for disputation had vanished. He nodded once, solemnly and it was as if I was nodding to myself after I had killed Stark, that single,

136

slow nod of approval in the darkness. Done it and done it good, you, I had murmured and had been speaking to myself, now too it had happened again except that this self was an extension. "Go," I said again, "go back to your people. Teach them. Teach them what we know so that they may become us."

"Yes," he said, that was all, just *yes* and then he turned. I hit the locks, I hit the pressure latches and slowly the skin of the ship broke open in pores of light, the inversion of sky pressing upon it and then he was gone, two steps and a leap. In that bound, falling clear of the ship I saw him framed as if in a still life, the features poised, rigid, as delicately formed as if they had been cast and when he had fallen out of the network of sight, he diminished below consciousness as well . . . and as he went away, as I turned to seal up the hatches again, thought of Ezekiel had already deserted me. I did not need to think of him any more; he would do as he must just as I would, soldered together we had been fissioned apart, but these parts would always know of the gestalt. At least that is the way that it seemed. Perhaps I was suppressing my very deep and genuine emotions at a great loss.

But the ship was sealed, Ezekiel was gone and I turned then in the emptiness to perform the few, small tasks that were left me before, necessarily, all of my responsibilities would end. And not a moment too soon.

XIX

AWAKENESS: But I must have known it all the time, the thought like a battered flower coming from the bruised earth of the consciousness, I had stamped that flower, spat on it, raked it under layers of mud but it had been there all of the time and I knew it: storming from sleep in the tube where I lay, wrenched from the abcess of sleep I had come to consciousness borne by jolt after jolt of pain, the pain like fire in the body but seeming extrinsic to it as well as if body and tubing had been joined; the aqueous sac in which we slept was the conductor, filaments were thrown between body and tubing in the sac so that not only I but the ship was in pain, the ship me, I the ship, joined and jolted in flare after flare and as I rushed from the core of unconsciousness it was with the unalterable knowledge that something had gone wrong.

We might have been struck by some disturbance in the ether (I know nothing of space; the training processes told me only how to handle the crew and the stresses of the ship; space to me is an abstraction) which I could not understand, some gigantic compression or hand in space might have seized and squeezed us, perhaps it had been something for which we had no language at all; but as I tore myself to consciousness, like a beetle moving through layers of wood, it was this knowledge of irreplaceable loss that came atop the pain.

Pain and loss, loss and pain, the one felt, the other merely a constriction, but even as I tried to get out of the sac and deal with it, I had to lay back while the revivifying equipment, on automatic to my coming to consciousness, worked me over, massaging the body, restoring the mind, slowly elevating the respiration and circulation and it must have been twenty minutes, more than that, before I could stagger out of the tank and into the other equipment which cleaned and dressed me; it must have been more time after that until I was able finally to come into the sitting room of the ship and look out upon the heavens, the glaring and naked heavens, the unfamiliar stars pieced out in constellations for which we had no name, the ship reeling drunkenly in relation to those stars so that they appeared in right port, left port and center, the abscissa of the ship's flight cutting new patterns and then, as I stared, blinking, charging long-departed moisture into my eyes, the heavens rolled once again, the deadly churning of the ship setting up complex patterns of nausea and retching and I grasped toward the bars, then righted myself as slowly the ship rotated in its course on a three hundred and sixty degree angle, moving not only parallel but centrifugal then to the universe and as it turned . . .

. . . As it turned the ship passed through a certain pattern at one hundred and twenty degrees which was familiar, the stars suddenly reordering themselves, the new patterns becoming constellations which were recognizable and on the brink of that vision I gasped; the ship was turning away then, at one hundred and forty degrees the pattern was already ruptured, at one hundred and eighty it was reassembled into something entirely different, a parody of what I had seen but that afterimage burned itself upon the retinas of my weary, barely reconstituted commander's eyes and seeing it there I experienced a gasping moment of understanding in which I saw everything, knew then what had happened to us but the fracturing roll split the heavens apart and I staggered from the porthole, then tried to deny what I had seen, refusing it, reordering it into something else, but, then as I . . .

. . . Reeled back to my commander's couch the

139

vision was still there, the constellations reordered at a hundred and twenty degrees and I knew what had happened, I must have known it in sleep (sleep tossing me back toward that consumation of knowledge which waking had destroyed) and still I did not want to phrase it, did not want to bring it to the mind, a mind that was waxen from months behind the penitentiary of coma and so I suppressed it, put it below the shelf of consciousness not to be rummaged with and went to check on the rooms of my sleeping companions. In one room was Nina and in another was Stark and in the third was Closter just as I had remembered, each was immersed in the tanks, their bodies dark as fish under the surface of the water, the waters lapping, all peaceful, all of them . . . even the one that should have been waking was peaceful and knowing this I nodded once slightly, inhaling the odors of their sleep and then went back to my own place where I lay and rested and thought for a long time . . .

. . . Knowing that one of them was sleeping like a cheat, that instead of remaining awake as the fool should have done, the fool had cheated, refused to yield the biological clock and had placed himself in sleep once again and it was during this sleep that the lurch had come which was to wrench me from my own depths and I could not . . .

. . . Could not remember who it was supposed to be on alert, coma having purged so much from my mind; a simple glance at the logs in the deck would show me which of the three was the liar but I did not want to look. I could not bring myself to do that, lying instead that way . . .

. . . And knew what had happened to us, knew that that shock of dislocation meant this: that we had been thrown not out in space but back in *time,* that dislocative thrill which went to the root of the stalk of the unconscious, had cast us back in time causing us to fall deep into the pit of space and that the constellations I had seen were not foreign but were the familiar patterns of our Earth twisted by the ship's dive through that opening in time momentarily out of focus, only to reassemble with the turning of the ship . . .

. . . Knew then that we were not journeying out but merely *back* in time, the knowledge coming upon me with the horrid conviction and certainty with which, a long time after that, I had buried myself deep into Nina, into Stark, into Closter lest they find out what I knew and that what we were going to meet at the end of that voyage when the ship fell was not Folsom's Planet at all but rather a prehistoric *Earth* and that we would be reconstructing to these barbarians all of our known history, that we might, in fact, *be* our history and let me tell you, gentlemen, this certainty . . .

. . . This absolute, thundering, certainty . . .

. . . Well, it is the kind of thing that might have driven a man mad if he had known it to be true, if he had accepted it, gentlemen, it would drive even the best of you mad, let alone the commander of this humble craft, the humble Hans Folsom, himself a man not unacquainted with sorrows or unfamiliar to grief who was hardly prepared to put up with stresses of this nature . . .

. . . Would, as I say, have driven better people than Folsom mad if they had accepted it, the conundrum that is: that he and his crew would have become their own *biblical ancestors because of this fall through the warp in time,* but fortunately for you, to say nothing of Folsom himself, fortunately for each and for everyone of us, Folsom refused to accept the fact that anything as bizarre as this could possibly be true and therefore he absolutely refused to accept it knowing that it was merely an insane delusion: there was no warp in time, there was no founder in the ship, there was merely the highly disturbed Folsom himself and his difficult relationship with situations which he could not understand and therefore . . . well, therefore, gentlemen, Folsom was not driven insane at all; Folsom denied all of this and was able to function quite well despite his period of uncer-

141

tanity in the ship alone with the sleepers and the cheating sleeper . . . although, now that this has been revealed, you can understand quite well why Folsom might have been driven to precipitate action by the naming of the alien *Ezekiel*. Surely that is fully understandable.

But otherwise his conduct is beyond reproach.

I am sure that even by your own rigorous terms, this will explain everything.

XX

FLICKER OF HISTORY: When the alien is gone, when the locks are sealed up again, when he is alone and at last in possession of the great ship, Folsom sends back a message to the recalcitrant Bureau which did not understand him and refused to cooperate even after he told them the truth of the mission and what had happened to them. The message was extraordinarily obscene and bears no place in the memoirs of a true spaceman and hero and is therefore omitted. Not to be paraphrased, either. I am sure that you will understand this: Folsom is sure as well, the two of us share this assurance. It had something to do, it can be hinted, with his real opinion of the Bureau.

Having done this, Folsom then sealed the ship in a final and devastating fashion, using certain emergency devices which were specifically to be utilized only in a state of the most absolute emergency such as attack by aliens, combustion of the planet, murderous attacks by fellow crew members, etc. Ordinarily these protective means are supposed to be secret, even from the commander, but Folsom was energetic and cunning and had a great captain's heart so they were not. Secret from him that is.

Standing then at the porthole, looking out at the aspect of his world from the high place of the nose cone where he could see beyond the forest into the clearing, standing there and seeing the village in little off-flickers of vision, Folsom thought for a moment that he could see the natives gathered to celebrate their knowledge, thought that if he could only extend his vision that perilous last foot or so toward insight he would see exactly what use they would make of his knowledge but in the next moment he knew that it was all hallucinatory and that he saw nothing else, was looking, if anywhere, only at the scarred interior of his own, great, ruined heart: seeing this Folsom felt a flaming leap of insight unlike any that he had ever quite known, the insight painting his view of the world in many colors bright and dark and he leapt to embrace it; with the insight flaring then within he wrestled for a long, long time with it and lesser mysteries until at last, with a roar, his magnificent, grizzled, leader's heart imploded upon him, little slivers of fragmentation puncturing his soul like ash . . . and there he lay, stretched across the destruct button that he did not quite have the will to push—because it would have destroyed the very future that he had, the only memory that he knew—for quite a while but eventually it was time to do something else and Folsom did it. Did the necessary. Although what it is, it is rather impossible to say; the Bureau being rather out of touch on this most ancient and terrible of topics.